Wyatt's eyes twinkled. "We're a proud lot."

"I've heard as much."

With his finger, he pushed a barrel curl resting on her cheek behind her ear. From the second his finger glided across her skin, ridiculous yearning reared up again, putting a halt to their pleasant banter. He gazed at her with dire want, his eyes dipping down to her mouth.

"Brooke," he rasped. There was a distinct hitch in his voice that touched something powerful inside her quivering belly.

"It's okay, Wyatt," she said. Whatever he wanted, she was ready for.

A groan rose from his throat and he began shaking his head as if he couldn't believe what was happening. One of his hands wrapped firmly around her waist, his fingers inching her closer, while the other hand was lifting her chin. His lips met hers. She felt instantly safe with Wyatt, and it wasn't borne by his saving her from empty gas tanks or pesky older men. It was something more, something she'd never experienced before. Utter trust.

* * *

Twins for the Texan
is part of Mills & Boon Desire's Nº1 bestselling series, Billionaires and Babies: Powerful men… wrapped around their babies' little fingers.

TWINS FOR THE TEXAN

BY
CHARLENE SANDS

MILLS & BOON

First Published in Great Britain 2016
By Mills & Boon, an imprint of HarperCollins*Publishers*
1 London Bridge Street, London, SE1 9GF

© 2016 Charlene Swink

ISBN: 978-0-263-26430-2

Charlene Sands is a *USA TODAY* bestselling author of more than forty romance novels, writing sensual contemporary romances and stories of the Old West. When not writing, Charlene enjoys sunny Pacific beaches, great coffee, reading books from her favorite authors and spending time with her family. You can find her on Facebook and Twitter, write her at PO Box 4883, West Hills, CA 91308, or sign up for her newsletter for fun blogs and ongoing contests at charlenesands.com.

To my sweet mother-in-law, Nancy, with love.
Thanks for having twins, inspiring this story
and giving me a great husband!

One

Brooke McKay had no clue where this deserted Texas road was taking her. Gazing past a dozen squished bugs on the rental car's windshield, she saw flatland stretching before her for miles and miles. After living in California near mountains and beaches, this kind of vast flatness was foreign to her.

Red warning lights blinked from the car's dashboard. She looked down at the indicator. Her gas tank was nearing empty. "Don't do it, don't do it."

Decked out in her best black lace dress with all the necessary trimmings and red heels so high they'd put the balls of her feet to the test in the walking-to-the-next-gas-station department, Brooke pushed the car to its limit.

She spotted something lying in the middle of the road. "Oh!"

Roadkill.

Apparently someone had driven on this road recently. It was good news for her, but not for the poor possum.

As she drove on, she removed her sunglasses and squinted into the afternoon sun searching for a miracle. A gas station would be nice, with an attendant who knew where in heck she was.

The car sputtered, the engine wringing out its last breaths.

She sucked in oxygen, praying that her worst nightmare wasn't coming to life.

And then the car crawled to a stop.

She pumped the gas pedal, but there was no more wringing to be had.

Oh, boy. Not only wouldn't she make it to Heather's wedding on time, she might have to camp out here in the wilderness for heaven knew how long.

She stared at her cell phone lying beside her on the seat. She already knew *that* miracle wasn't happening. She had no cell service. She hadn't for the last ten miles. She knocked her head against the leather steering wheel a few times and decided it made a good pillow, a place to rest her head and close her eyes while she thought of a way out of this predicament. She didn't have many choices. She'd have to get out and start walking.

"Excuse me, miss," came a deep voice from out of nowhere. "Are you okay?"

Her head popped up, and she looked into the bone-melting blue eyes of the man standing beside her driver-side door. Her heartbeat immediately picked up speed. There in the flesh was a dauntingly handsome, iron-jawed cowboy.

Her miracle.

"I, uh, I didn't hear anyone drive up." She glanced in her rearview mirror and sure enough, a shiny black Cadillac SUV was parked behind her car. "Yes, yes. I'm okay."

She took a closer look at him. Goodness, they grew them tall in Texas. Her miracle wore a black Western suit, a sterling silver belt buckle and one of those sexy string ties. "I th-think I took a wrong turn somewhere. Now I'm out of gas."

He nodded and scrubbed at the dark blond facial hair on his jaw. "Not a good thing to do on this road. There isn't a gas station for at least ten miles or so. I'm Wyatt Brandt, by the way." He stuck out his hand and she took it. It was a little awkward shaking hands through the car window, but his firm grip, beautiful eyes and rich Texas drawl put her at ease.

He could be a serial killer.

That thought flittered through her mind, but she dismissed it. The butterflies winging around in her stomach as he enveloped her hand, ever so briefly, told a different story. "I'm Brooke. I was heading to a friend's wedding, and now I'm afraid I'll never make it."

"Nice meeting you, Brooke," he said. "You wouldn't by any chance be heading to Blake and Heather's shindig, would you?"

Her eyebrows drew up. How did he know? *Serial killer* flashed in her mind again. Had he been stalking her? Her brother Dylan had almost lost his life to a stalker out to get revenge. Luckily, he'd survived the murder attempts and decided to get his wife away from the Hollywood scene for a while. Emma, Dylan and Brooke were all in Texas now, while Dylan was shooting a movie. She still had stalker on the brain but immediately dismissed the notion where Wyatt was concerned. How many stalkers drove Cadillacs and dressed like *GQ* models? No, Wyatt Brandt either was psychic or had been invited to the wedding, too. "Yes, that's the one. The GPS told me to take this road. I was running late, and this is supposed to be a shortcut to their wedding venue. Do you know them?"

"Sure do. I'm on my way to the nuptials, too. Blake's a friend of mine."

She smiled. This miracle was getting better and better.

"Heather and I went to college on the West Coast together. I've never met Blake."

"He's a great guy. Just so you know I'm not anyone you have to worry over. I own the Blue Horizon Ranch, about fifteen miles back that way." He pointed behind them. "And yes, this is a shortcut, if you know the roads. I'd be happy to give you a lift. I was running a bit late, too, and if we hurry, we'll make it before the ceremony begins."

"Gosh, that sounds great."

He opened the door for her and she got out. Their size difference was immediately evident. Even wearing three-inch heels, the top of her head reached his chin. His very rugged, strong chin.

"What about your car?" he asked.

"It's a rental." He closed the car door for her and she went on to explain, "I've been a little distracted lately, and forgot to fill the tank when I took off earlier. I'll lock it up and leave it here for now. I don't have much choice if I want to make the wedding."

He nodded. "Sounds good."

"Just let me get my bag." She clicked a button and the trunk popped open. He followed behind and before she could reach for her bag, he stretched a long arm around her, grazing her waist, and grabbed her suitcase. Warm shivers cascaded down her body from the contact. It was ridiculous how instantly attracted she was to him. She knew nothing about him other than his left hand was bare of a wedding ring and he had incredible eyes and pretty great manners.

"Anything else?" Her pink Gucci bag looked tiny in his grasp.

She'd heard about Southern charm, but experiencing it firsthand was refreshing. The men in other parts of the country could take a lesson from Wyatt Brandt. "No, that's it. Thank you."

"So you're staying overnight?" he asked as he guided her to his SUV.

"Yes. I figured the reception might go late, and I didn't think I'd be any good driving these roads at night. I'm not too great on them during the day either, apparently."

Rich laughter rose from his chest. "Probably a smart move." He opened the passenger-side door and she climbed into the seat.

Once she had settled in, she caught him gazing at her legs. A wave of heat passed through her as his eyes lingered just long enough not to be creepy.

After he put her suitcase in the back end, he took his seat behind the steering wheel and gave her a smile. "Do you have a last name?" he asked matter-of-factly as he started the engine. "Or are you just Brooke?"

Goodness, she didn't want to be Brooke McKay, not today, not with Wyatt. As soon as a guy got wind of who she really was, the sister of ultra-famous movie star Dylan McKay, he began treating her differently. She loved Dylan to pieces, but she'd had enough of that role, and it had caused her too much heartache with men who'd played her fast and loose just to get close to her famous brother.

Maybe it would be different in Texas than it had been in Los Angeles, where everyone it seemed, was trying to break into the movie business. But Brooke was too scarred now to test out that theory. "I'm Brooke *Johnson*."

The fib fell easily from her lips. For just one day. Was that asking too much?

"Okay, Brooke Johnson. Are you ready?"

"I think I was born ready," she said.

He laughed and they took off, leaving her little white Ford Escort in the dust.

Wyatt hadn't had a one-on-one conversation with a woman since his wife, Madelyn, had died some nine months ago. He wasn't including Henrietta in that, since his housekeeper was nearing retirement age, and besides, he was never really alone with her. Either Brett or Brianna or both of his eighteen-month-old twins were usually with them when they spoke, or rather when they tried to have a conversation. Raising twins was chaos in motion most of the time.

Yet Wyatt wasn't one for parties anymore. He preferred staying on the ranch, working long hours while trying to be a good father. But even he recognized his grief needed a swift kick in the ass, and his best friend Johnny Wilde had been the one to deliver it. "Go to that weddin', man. What you need is to get out and start livin' again."

Now he was wearing a monkey suit and heading for Blake's wedding, making conversation with a dark-haired woman with a sultry voice, great legs, and dark chocolate eyes with lids heavily shadowed and rims outlined in black.

"You're not from Texas, are you?" he asked.

"What was your first clue?"

He'd gotten a load of clues: the raven hair curling wildly down her back, the red painted lips, the dark made-up eyes and the manner of her dress. Sexy as it was, no woman in Texas would wear a skintight black lace dress to a wedding. At least none of the weddings he'd ever attended. "Oh, I don't know. Just a hunch."

"I'm from Los Angeles."

Her lips puckered as if she expected him to make some comment about her appearance. He wouldn't disrespect her that way. She was different from Madelyn, who'd been the epitome of Texas style and grace with sweet features, rosy cheeks and soft blond hair. Brooke certainly had her own style, but he wouldn't say she was unattractive. Quite the opposite, and he wished to hell he wasn't constantly noticing.

"So, you've come all this way for the wedding?" he asked.

"Yes, and for a little vacation. It just sort of worked out that I'd be able to attend Heather's wedding. I haven't seen her in years, but we've kept in touch. I'll be here for the rest of the summer."

"Where are you staying?"

"With a friend just outside of Beckon."

He nodded. "Nice."

"Yeah, it would be, but I co-own a business and I've put it in the hands of a new manager while I'm gone. It's a little nerve-racking."

"What kind of business?"

"It's called Parties-to-Go. We do all sorts of party and event planning. My partner is pregnant and well, it's a little complicated, but we both decided we needed a break. So we're here, enjoying the muggy end of the summer."

And he was enjoying her.

"What do you do, Wyatt? If you don't mind me asking? You said you owned Blue Horizon Ranch? Does that mean cattle?"

"Sure does. I've been raising cattle nearly all of my life. When my granddaddy started the ranch back in the forties, it was a small operation. My daddy built it up some, and then I took over when my folks moved to the East Coast. Blue Horizon's success had always been a dream of mine."

That and living to a ripe old age with his high school sweetheart, Madelyn.

"And now you're seeing it through."

"I am. The ranch does well, but I tinker in other things, too."

"Ah, you're an entrepreneur?"

"I suppose some might call me that."

He took pride in the investments he'd made in other companies that had paid off well. He'd made his first million before his twenty-seventh birthday, and he'd worked hard ever since to ensure a comfortable future for his family. Now he had all the money he'd ever need. Without Madelyn to share in his success, all of his hard work would've seemed pointless, but for his twins.

That was what getting off the ranch this weekend was about, him trying to move on with his life.

Start livin' again.

He glanced at Brooke, her red-lipped mouth in a pout as she tried to catch some cell service by waving her phone up in the air, putting it out the window for a few seconds. He couldn't seem to keep his eyes off her. She was a breath of fresh air and that alone stirred his juices. She was different and, he supposed, a lot of fun if he'd ever let himself find out.

"Nothing?" he asked once she gave up with her phone.

"Nope, not a blasted thing."

"We'll be at the hotel soon," he said.

The Inn at Sweetwater was known for lush gardens and scenic bridges along a natural lake. It was the destination spot for lovers and known as the ultimate venue for a romantic wedding. It was like the cherry topping on a hot fudge sundae for a bride and groom to speak their vows there. And it was why he'd resisted coming to this wedding.

Not on this day, of all days. It was Madelyn's birthday.

Hell, it was the exact reason Johnny insisted on his getting off the ranch. Wyatt needed the distraction, the time away. Wyatt had been restless and pensive and even Henrietta, bless her soul, had insisted he needed time to clear his head and gain some perspective. He'd be leaving his kids in her care overnight. Something he'd never done before, so with Johnny on his back and Henrietta pushing him, he'd accepted the invitation.

"What's wrong?" Brooke asked.

He turned to look into her pretty brown eyes. "Why do you think something's wrong?"

"Because I know you so well," she replied, grinning.

He laughed. "Sorry, just deep in thought."

"No apologies necessary. Aha! Finally, I'm getting bars on my cell. We must be nearing civilization. Excuse me while I call a tow service for my car."

"No problem." Wyatt listened to the deep, sensual lilt of her voice and tried to keep his eyes focused on the highway—not on Brooke Johnson, the engaging woman he'd picked up along the road.

As they drove through the intricate wrought iron gates of the venue, they entered a vibrant world of golf-course-green grass and tall swaying willows shading the lane leading up to the hotel. The Inn at Sweetwater was a plantation-style structure with palatial columns and snow-white shutters on every window. The gardens were ablaze with purple azaleas, pink peonies and stargazer lilies, and bluebonnets were interwoven among the stepping-stones. The paths all led to picturesque bridges arching over placid ponds. Off to the right fifty yards away, Sweetwater Lake sparkled in the late-afternoon sun.

"It looks like something out of a painting," Brooke said, hearing awe in her voice. She had an eye for creativity, and whoever landscaped these grounds knew how to set the mood. "Have you ever been here before?"

"No," Wyatt said. "But I've heard about it enough. It's my mother's favorite place. She'd have luncheons here with her friends."

"I can see why she'd like coming here."

Close to the lake's bank, there was a flowered canopy with descending wisteria vines waiting for the bride and groom. Hundreds of chairs tied with delicate satin bows were lined up in rows. Most of the guests were already seated.

Wyatt pulled the car up to a valet. And once they climbed out, he asked, "Want to make a run for it?"

"I think we have to. The wedding is supposed to start any minute."

"Okay, after you," he said, gesturing for her to take the lead.

She trotted along on her high heels, not an easy task even though the lush grass was as thick as a carpet. But after a few strides her heel dug into the rich earth and got stuck. Her leg twisted and she tipped sideways, stumbling. "Oh!"

Wyatt reached out and snagged her waist, catching her fall just in time.

"I've got you," he said, confidently. "You okay?"

They were locked together now, and her sensitive skin prickled under his touch. She liked being in his arms, and he seemed reluctant to let her go. A few seconds ticked by before he did.

"How many times are you going to save me today?" she asked breathlessly.

"As many as it takes," he offered, his blue eyes sparkling. She didn't know what to make of her miracle cowboy who'd caused her body to heat up with just one playful look. Was he teasing or flirting?

"I've got a solution to this problem," she said, snapping out of her insanity.

She slipped a finger into her shoes to pull at the straps and then wiggled out of them. Straightening, she came up holding her scarlet-red sandals between her fingers and nodded. "Okay, now I'm ready."

He blinked, grinned at her bare feet and then offered her his hand. They took off at a very brisk walk, making it to the last row of seats just seconds before the brides-maids began their trek down the aisle.

Brooke sighed in relief and sat back. A few minutes later, everyone in attendance rose to their feet as Heather glided down the aisle in an ivory satin wedding gown, her father walking beside her wearing a proud tearful smile. She held a gorgeous bouquet of new roses and fresh natural greenery that looked as though it had been handpicked just moments ago.

She met her handsome groom under the canopy, love shining in her eyes. Brooke looked on, happy for her friend who'd found love here in Texas. She'd probably start a family soon. Brooke's future wasn't quite so rosy. She didn't begrudge her friends, who'd already found happiness, but she'd always wondered what it was about her that seemed to repel any form of long-lasting relationship with a man. Being Dylan McKay's younger sister was like a noose around her neck. *Just hang me now,* she'd say to herself, whenever a man she'd dated starting hinting at meeting her celebrity brother. Of course, then came the teeny favors they'd ask of her.

Would your brother mind reading my script? I know it's gonna be a blockbuster.

I'm writing an autobiography and your brother would be perfect to star in the movie.

I'm starting a new business venture. I'm sure Dylan would love to get in on the ground floor once you tell him about it.

Riiiight.

Brooke was fed up with men who used her for their own personal gain. Leaving LA when she did had been a necessity. After the debacle with Royce Brisbane, who'd kept his cards close to the vest, and only showed his hand once she'd fallen in love with him, she'd written off relationships for the extended future. She'd been convinced her Wall Street–type boyfriend didn't give a lick about Dylan, until he handed her three scripts for her to show him. *Three*, for heaven's sake!

No man would ever use her that way again.

And then there was Wyatt Brandt, the polite, mannerly cowboy whose presence beside her made her heart pound in her chest. She didn't want to be Brooke McKay today, not while Wyatt Brandt was stealing glances at her when he didn't think she was looking. But she'd noticed, and it boosted her deflated ego to have a gorgeous hunk of a man checking her out without an ulterior motive. And if the tingles she was experiencing now weren't one-sided, this wedding could prove intriguing.

The *I do*'s were said with a flourish, and Brooke teared up as she witnessed these two people in love speak vows of undying commitment to each other. She felt Wyatt's eyes on her as a sole tear dripped down her cheek. Did he think her foolish for crying at a wedding? How cliché. Brooke wasn't a traditional kind of girl, yet weddings always seemed to get to her.

Wyatt gently placed a handkerchief in her hand. As she dabbed at her eyes, she sent him a silent nod of thanks. He gave her a brief smile.

After the vows were spoken, the loving couple garnered a round of applause as they marched down the aisle hand in hand, newly married. Row upon row of guests made their way from their seats to head toward the tented area where the cocktail hour was about to begin.

Brooke and Wyatt, seated in the back row, stood up and waited patiently for their turn. "It was a beautiful ceremony," she said, handing him his handkerchief.

"It was. But it made you cry."

She shrugged and slight embarrassment heated her skin. "I'm silly that way. Most people don't think of me as the sentimental type, but I guess I am when it comes to weddings."

"Maybe that's why you enjoy your business so much. You like seeing other people happy."

She stared into his eyes. Was he for real? How did he know that about her, after only meeting her two hours ago? Was he psychic after all? "You amaze me," she blurted.

"I do?" He rubbed at the scruffy dark blond hairs on his chin. "Well, now, it's been a while since I've amazed a woman."

"Don't stop on my account. It's been *too* long since I've been amazed by a man."

The look in his eyes suddenly grew dark and intense. "You flirting with me, Brooke Johnson?"

Yes. It was hard not to.

She glanced away for a second, making note of the two-hundred-plus guests milling about the large white wedding tent, and suddenly all she wanted was to be alone with Wyatt Brandt again.

"Just stating a fact, Wyatt."

"C'mon," he said, tamping down a smile and taking her arm gently. "Let's see if Blake and Heather had the good sense to seat us together."

She liked the sound of that.

A lot.

Two

Brooke wasn't seated with Wyatt. She sat between two of Heather's female cousins she'd met once or twice back in college. Two other male cousins and their wives rounded out the table. Everyone was pleasant. The ladies, dressed in florals and pastels appropriate for a late-afternoon wedding, were doing their best to make small talk. Brooke engaged in conversation with them and sipped white wine while giving the entire lakeside reception a cursory scan, keeping her eyes peeled for signs of Wyatt.

During the cocktail hour, she'd spent time with him, munching on appetizers and enjoying Sweetwater Lake until dinner had been called and they'd had to go their separate ways. She sensed that Wyatt had been just as disappointed as she was to discover that not only weren't they seated together, but their tables were separated by twenty others.

She spotted Wyatt standing just outside the perimeter of the decorated tent, sipping whiskey from a tumbler as he spoke to the groom. The sight of Wyatt shouldn't have made her heart race, and yet it was sprinting as if in an Olympic event. The two men shook hands and then Blake took off, most likely in search of his bride. Two women took Blake's place, sidling up next to Wyatt with giddy smiles on their faces.

She felt something possessive deep in her belly. He wasn't her date, but he seemed to want to spend more time with her, and now it didn't look as if that was going to happen.

Brooke's attention snapped back to her table when Connie, the younger of Heather's cousins, asked her a question. "Yes, I'm enjoying my stay in Texas so far," Brooke replied. "And I'm happy I was able to attend Heather's wedding. It was a beautiful ceremony."

"Heather's very happy with Blake. He's one of the good guys."

"There are so few of those," Brooke said, recognizing her tone was too cynical for a wedding.

Luckily, Connie chuckled. "I know what you mean. My mama says if you find a good one, land him and never let him go."

"She's a smart woman."

"She should know, she's been married three times. She kicked two losers to the curb before marrying my daddy. They've been married twenty-eight years now."

"I like your mother more and more."

"What about your folks?" Connie asked.

"Oh, my biological parents have issues. I don't see them much, but I was raised by foster parents and they were awesome. Without them, my life wouldn't be what it is today."

"So there's hope out there. I shouldn't be so skeptical— especially at my cousin's wedding—but my boyfriend and I have just broken up and it still stings."

She caught sight of Wyatt finally taking his seat for dinner. "I get the stinging part, Connie. I've been there." More than once. "It gets better, believe me. Just concentrate on what you enjoy doing most. That's what I do."

"Heather said you could've put this wedding together without blinking an eye."

"Heather is too kind, but if I lived here, yes, I would've loved to work on this event. There's so much natural beauty that only the fine points need accenting, and the event planner did a terrific job of not going overboard. I would've done the same."

"I guess that's the reason the inn is perfect for a wedding. It doesn't need too many added frills."

Dinner was served, toasts were given and the reception continued on smoothly. Brooke dug into her meal, enjoying the perfectly seasoned and cooked salmon, quinoa salad and freshly grilled veggies. The meal was light and tasty, and after she was finished and her plate was being cleared, a band began to make noises as they set up on a platform stage.

"Excuse me," she said to the guests at the table. She rose and walked over to the sweetheart table. This was the first chance she'd gotten to congratulate Heather and her new groom. After the ceremony, they'd been inundated by a swarm of well-meaning guests and Brooke hadn't entered the fray, deciding to bide her time until she could have a quiet conversation with the newlyweds.

"Heather, congratulations!" Brooke's friend rose and they immediately embraced.

"Brooke, my goodness, I'm so glad you were able to make it to our wedding. Blake," she said, turning to him, "I'd like you to meet my friend from Los Angeles. We went to UCLA together, back in the day."

Blake stood up and took her hand. "Nice meeting you, Brooke, and thanks for being here."

"It's a special day and I'm glad I could make it. Heather has been trying to get me to make a trip to Texas for years."

"Oh, yeah? I hope you're getting a big Texas welcome."

"I am. Everyone's been gracious and nice. I'm on vacation, staying with friends in Beckon, so I'll be here for several more weeks."

"That's wonderful," Heather said. "Maybe we can get together when Blake and I get back from our honeymoon."

"I'm taking her on a cruise of the Mediterranean. We'll be gone ten days."

"Sounds perfect. And I'd love to see you when you return. Heather, you look stunning and it's not just the gown...you're glowing. Blake must be doing something right," Brooke said, giving him a wink.

"You know it." Blake took Heather's hand. "I like your friend already."

"I told you you would," Heather said.

The master of ceremonies called for the newlyweds' first dance. "Well, I guess you're on, you two. Congratulations again. I'll speak to you later."

A crowd formed around the parquet dance floor set up under the glorious white tent. Brooke took a position in the outer circle as the two lovebirds danced to a George Strait ballad. The lights were dimmed, and a sole spotlight shone on them like a halo. Heather really was glowing now.

Once the dance was over, there was a round of applause, and the bandleader urged the guests to join the bride and groom on the dance floor. Brooke headed to her table. Before she reached her seat, a man approached. He was in his midforties, she guessed, his tie crooked, his entire body seemingly angled to the left, as if he'd fall over any second. "W-would...you like to d-dance?"

His breath reeked of alcohol. "Uh, no thank you."

"Just one dance, missy, is all I'm asking."

"No, thank you," Brooke said as politely as she could

manage. She turned away from him and started for her table again. But he snagged her arm from behind, thick fingers digging deep into her skin. She whirled on him and yanked her arm free. "What part of no don't you get?" she said quietly. The last thing she wanted was to make a scene at Heather's wedding.

"You're a f-feisty little th-thing." He reached for her again and it was easy to step out of his grasp.

"And you've obviously had too much to drink."

"Is there a problem here?" Wyatt got between her and the pesky man, towering a good six inches above the guy. Wyatt's glare made it clear he wasn't one to mess with.

The man leaned way over, nearly toppling, and Wyatt quickly caught him.

"No p-problem. Nope. N-not a one," he said, chuckling.

"I think you need some air." Wyatt held the man upright and turned to Brooke, his mouth twisting in a smirk. He winked at her. "I'll be back as soon as I can."

He escorted—or rather supported—the guy out of the tent and Brooke returned to her seat. The man was probably harmless, but Brooke didn't like being manhandled that way. She'd been ready to raise her voice and call security, which would've dampened the festive mood. Once again, Wyatt was there, stepping in to save the day.

A quiet hum strummed through her body and she smiled.

"That's weird Uncle Hal," Connie said into her ear as Brooke lowered down into the chair beside her. "I caught some of what happened out there and my whole family apologizes to you." Connie made a face. "Hal likes to drink…when the liquor is free. Heather almost didn't invite him to the wedding. She was afraid he'd cause a scene. But he seems to have been neutralized."

"Neutralized?"

"Yeah, once he's been set straight, he doesn't cause any more trouble. He'll probably come over to say he's sorry."

"I hope not." Brooke shivered.

"Who was that hunk who took him outside?"

"Oh, um, he's a friend of the groom's. I met him earlier today."

"Does he have a younger brother, if you know what I mean?"

Brooke sighed. "Yeah, I do know what you mean. And honestly, I don't know."

"You're three for three, Wyatt," Brooke said.

Wyatt held her at arm's length as they danced to a light and breezy love song. His touch, though highly appropriate, thrilled her from head to toe. There was something steady and sturdy about him. He made her feel female, which seemed silly, but those deep blue eyes studied her with keen intent, as if she were a secret art treasure or a delicious hot fudge sundae. Either way, she was happy to be the object of his attention.

"How's that?" he asked.

"You saved me thrice, my lord," she said with a mock curtsy. "The last time with big Uncle Hal."

He laughed. "You were handling the situation just fine."

"You think so?"

"I do. But I also saw the indecision on your face. Where I come from, a man doesn't lay a hand on a woman 'less he's invited. When he didn't back down I figured you didn't want to make a scene."

"You're right about that. I don't like to draw attention to myself."

He drew her closer and spoke into her ear softly, "Then you shouldn't have worn that dress."

His gaze dipped past the lace on her scooped neckline

and touched upon her breasts. From under the material, her nipples tightened. Wyatt could do that to her with one look.

"You don't like it?" she asked, a little uncertain. "Or was that a compliment?"

Emma, her bestie, business partner and sister-in-law, was always telling her to put some color in her wardrobe, but black was her thing. She wasn't a floral kind of girl.

"Every guy in this place has his sights set on you. And I'm the one dancing with you." Appreciation shone in his eyes and she almost forgot all about Royce what's-his-name. "I like it, all right."

"Thank you."

"Welcome." His hands snaked around her waist, and the space between them lessened to inches. Brooke wasn't complaining. He smelled like whiskey and something woodsy and natural. She took deep breaths of him, drinking in his scent and enjoying the way his dark blond hair curled at his collar.

"I have a confession," he said in a quiet rasp. "I'm glad your car ran out of gas today."

Something broke apart inside her then, and her cynicism crumbled away. At least for the present, she wasn't going to question her actions. Or his. This perfect guy seemed to come straight out of her dreams, and she wasn't going to play it safe tonight. Not with Wyatt. She brought her fingers to the curls at the back of his neck and smiled, titling her chin up. Her eyes had to be gleaming now. "I'm glad, too," she said.

Wyatt's gaze heated. Thrills ran up and down her spine as she waited for him to do something bold, something daring.

He brought his head closer, never losing eye contact with her. "Are you inviting me?" he said, but he didn't wait for her answer. The connection they had was real and happening fast. He had to feel it, too.

His lips brushed hers softly, once, twice. Shock waves traveled the length of her body. She hadn't realized how much she'd needed this, how much she'd missed the simple reality of connecting with a man on an elemental level. The pure masculine taste of him washed completely through her, and a soft purr escaped her lips. She kissed him back and things got hot and heavy really fast. He cupped the back of her head, weaving fingers through her long, wild hair. "Oh, man," he murmured, pressing his lips more forcefully to hers, making exquisite demands on her. Demands she was eager to answer.

Was it lust? She'd been attracted to Wyatt from the second she'd laid her eyes on him. And now he was kissing her as if he'd been starving, and let's face it, she hadn't even nibbled in a very long time. Now she was ravenous.

Wyatt broke off the kiss before things got completely out of control on the dance floor and sighed loud enough for her to hear his frustration. Her ego was lifted to new heights as he tugged her tightly into his embrace, pressing their bodies closer. The slow ballad continued, but she barely heard the music. All she knew, all she felt, was her connection to Wyatt. They were so close, so incredibly in tune with each other.

Tension sizzled between them in a crazy way that upset her newly regained balance. She wasn't ready for this, for him. But when the dance ended and he stared into her eyes, she was lost.

"Let's get some air, darlin'."

She gave him a tiny nod, and he grabbed her hand and tugged her toward the edge of the draped tent that led to the lake.

Soft blades of grass tickled her ankles as Wyatt wove a path to the bank of Sweetwater Lake. Moonlight reflected off the rippling waters now, the sun having long ago bid farewell to the day. The air was still damp with humidity, but since sunset the temperature had cooled considerably. They stood facing the lake.

"Better," he said, taking gulps of air into his lungs. "It got a little heavy in there."

He dropped her hand, seeming to compose himself.

"It did."

"You surprised me, is all," he said, looking away from the lake to connect with her again. "I mean, I didn't expect..."

"I know. I'm different." He didn't have to say it. He didn't expect to be attracted to her. "I'm no Texas girl. I dress weird most of the time. Believe it or not, I toned it down for the wedding." No leather wrist bracelets, giant hoop earrings or multiple long chains around her neck for this shindig. As a matter of fact, she'd left most of that stuff back home in LA. Maybe she was entering a new phase in her life.

"I like your style, Brooke. There's nothing weird about you."

"Thanks for that."

"I mean it. When I saw you with Uncle Hal on the dance floor, I had an irrational urge to knock his block off."

"Is that equivalent to punching his lights out?"

"It is," he stated plainly.

"Why, Wyatt, that's the nicest thing anyone's ever said to me." She stood toe-to-toe with him, grinning. It felt good to break the tension and get back to easy conversation with him.

He laughed loud and deep and she joined in, too.

"I like you, Brooke," he said easily.

"Feeling's mutual," Brooke said. "Isn't that how they say it out here?"

"Stop poking fun at Texans." Wyatt's eyes twinkled. "We're a proud lot."

"I've heard as much."

A wicked Texas breeze blew strands of hair into her face.

With his finger, Wyatt innocently pushed a barrel curl resting on her cheek behind her ear. From the second his finger glided across her skin, the ridiculous yearning reared up again, putting a halt to their pleasant banter. Her laughter died in her throat, and as she focused on the man touching her tenderly, his smile changed into something less animated and playful. He gazed at her with dire want, his eyes dipping down to her pursed and needy mouth.

"Brooke," he rasped. There was a distinct hitch in his voice.

"It's okay, Wyatt," she said. Whatever he wanted, she was ready for.

A groan rose from his throat and he began shaking his head as if he couldn't believe what was happening. Brooke was in the same boat. They were sailing along at break-neck speed. She wasn't about to throw down the anchor; she wanted the wind at her back taking her wherever this was leading.

Wyatt wrapped one of his hands firmly around her waist, his fingers inching her closer, while he lifted her chin to meet his beautiful giving mouth with the other. The kiss was sweeter, more leisurely than before. She instantly felt safe with Wyatt; it wasn't about his saving her from empty gas tanks or pesky older men. It was something more, something she'd never experienced before. Utter trust.

The little voice in her head said, *It's because he doesn't know who you really are.*

But that wasn't it. A Texas rancher couldn't care less about her being a celebrity's sister. Wyatt had no agenda in that regard, and this uncanny faith she had in him came from a deeper, more soulful place within her.

Only seconds later, Wyatt whispered a curse over her lips and deepened the kiss, making it hard for Brooke to think straight. Helpless to curtail the sizzling connection between them, she flung her arms around his neck and his kisses immediately became inferno hot. Her lips were on fire, set ablaze by this amazingly strong, gorgeous man. He walked her backward until she met with the solid breadth of a cottonwood tree. She leaned against it, out of view of the wedding tent and the two hundred other guests.

He urged her mouth open and their tongues tangled. Explosive sensations rocked her back and a potent stream of desire coursed through her body, making her feel more alive than she'd felt in a long, long time. Wyatt had her trapped, his arms on either side of the thick tree. There wasn't any place else she'd rather be.

He brought his arms down to cup her face and tilted her head at an angle that was to his liking. His kiss was more deliberate this time, packed with intensity and precision. Oh, he was a yummy kisser.

He began an exploration of her body with both hands grazing her shoulders and traveling down her sides, along the inward curve of her torso and caressing the slight flare of her hips. She could tell he wanted to touch her in more intimate places but his keen sense of propriety wouldn't allow it. She wanted more, but couldn't deny how incredibly sweet and sensitive he was to her.

They came up for air a minute later, both shaking, both completely turned on. The music inside the tent stopped and the bandleader's gleeful voice carried over the microphone, announcing it was time for the bride and groom to cut the cake.

"Brooke." He whispered her name on a sigh and touched his forehead to hers, his warm breath caressing her cheek. "We should really go back inside."

"Mmm." He was right, of course, but how on earth would she stop her legs from trembling, her body from quivering? "I think so, too."

"You go first," he said, encouraging her with a nod. "I'll need a minute. Oh, and be sure to save the last dance for me."

She straightened her disheveled dress, took a swallow, steadied her out-of-whack nerves and then headed up the embankment toward the tent. Halfway there, she swiveled her head around to find Wyatt's discerning eyes still on her.

She turned to continue her trek, purring with quiet delight like a kitten lapping up a bowl of rich cream.

"Here you go," Wyatt said so quietly she barely heard him. He set her luggage down outside her hotel room door as she slid the key card into the lock.

"Thank you," she said, turning to him. "I, um, had a great time tonight. The wedding was pretty cool."

"I had a good time, too. Thanks to you."

She stared at him, quaking inside. She didn't want to make another mistake. But looking into Wyatt's eyes, she didn't believe him to be one. "You give me too much credit."

"I don't think so. I was dreading coming here today. And then I met you."

She blinked. He had a way of saying the right things. He wasn't a clever charmer, but he was charming. And he was a gentleman, in every way that counted. "Why were you dreading it?"

Pain entered his eyes. "Let's just say I'm new to bachelorhood and leave it at that."

"Oh." She got that. She didn't want to rehash her past relationships, either. One of the best parts of meeting Wyatt tonight was not having to think about the Royce Brisbanes of the world. She was fine with forgetting all about her own lousy relationships. "Okay."

Wyatt tilted his head. "You're not like most women."

"That doesn't sound like a compliment, Wyatt."

"Believe me, it is. Most women want to nose around and fix what's broken, but I'm not into that right now."

He was broken? Now that was a revelation, because from where she stood all of his parts seemed to be in excellent working order. "Wyatt," she said softly. She didn't want him to leave. Gosh, how she didn't want to say good-night to him.

"I'd better get to my room."

She didn't miss the reluctance in his voice. "Okay. Thanks for being my miracle cowboy today."

He blinked, seemingly surprised at her comment.

She smiled and lifted up on tiptoes to brush a soft kiss to his cheek.

He kissed her back, a gentle peck on the mouth. "Welcome."

She loved the taste of him, the way he smelled, the sturdy breadth of him.

He gazed at her mouth, his eyes holding a lingering dark gleam as if he wanted more. As if he wanted to devour her. The bone-melting effect reached all the way down to the tips of her toes. If he touched her again, she would be lost.

And then he did just that. He splayed his hands on her waist and drew her closer. "I need one more kiss, Brooke."

His rich baritone voice did crazy things to her, especially when he was asking to kiss her again. *Oh, man.* "Anything you need." Her voice was a breathless whisper.

And then their mouths came together in an amazing onslaught of potency and possession. Heat immediately rose up and flared like a lit match. It was as if everything fell into place again. His hands wound tighter around her waist. Her arms wrapped around his neck. Their lips smacked, and moans and sweet sighs of pleasure surrounded them.

"Take it inside, you two," a passerby said, chuckling as

he headed down the hallway, obviously having had one too many.

"Good idea," Wyatt stated softly over her lips.

"Yes, Wyatt. Yes."

With one hand, he pushed the heavy door open and then lifted her luggage and plunked it down just inside the room. Then the door closed behind him and they were alone in the dark hotel room.

"Just tell me you want this," he said, bracing her against the wall.

"I want this."

"God, Brooke. You're the one who's the miracle."

It was the sweetest, most beautiful thing anyone had ever said to her. She squeezed her eyes closed briefly and drank it all in. She drank *him* all in, too. His kisses set her body on fire, and now that they were out of the public eye, they were free to unleash their passion full force.

"I need to touch you," he whispered.

"Touch me."

His palms traveled over the slopes and curves of her body. His hands were large and rough, but he was gentle in his approach, making her want him all the more. He lifted her leg up under the knee, and she gasped as he slid his hand under the tight confines of her dress, stroking her thigh back and forth, over and over. "You're soft," he murmured between kisses. His body pressed to hers was a wall of granite, so big and hard, and she was overwhelmed with sensation after sensation. Between her thighs, pulsing heat gathered and her breaths came in short, rapid bursts.

He lowered her leg to the floor and flipped her around to face the wall, her back to his front. He probed her backside, skimming his hands over black lace. Through the material of her dress, the heat of his palms scorched her skin and she sighed, surrendering her body to him.

Finally, he inched the zipper of her dress down. She felt

the cooling fresh air on her skin as he pushed her dress away. Planting kisses on her shoulders, he undid her bra and then reached around to cup her breasts. He filled his hands, massaging and caressing her until she could barely stand the pleasure, tiny moans escaping her lips.

He skimmed his hands down her torso and back up again, navigating her body as if he were exploring points on a map. "You're soft everywhere."

She loved the quiet words he spoke over her shoulder and the way he held her so preciously. She breathed in the aroused scent of him as he reclaimed her aching breasts, his body pressed to hers, fully aroused, his scent intoxicating.

"We need to move this onto the bed," he said. "Unless you like—"

"No, the bed is fine," she managed.

He helped her remove the remainder of her clothes and then lifted her into his strong arms. He carried her to the turned-down bed and laid her there carefully.

Without saying a word, he kicked off his shoes and undressed for her, undoing his string tie, removing his jacket, shirt, belt and pants.

From what she could see from the sliver of moonlight streaming into the window, Wyatt met and exceeded her expectations. God, he was glorious above the waist, with brick shoulders and hard abs. And below, well, she took a huge gulp. He was definitely all man.

"Don't ask me why," he said, quite earnestly, "but I have protection."

"That's a relief," she said softly. "I don't."

She hadn't exactly planned on hitting the jackpot tonight, but she thought it odd that he would be apologizing for carrying protection. He'd said he was new to bachelorhood. She assumed he was divorced, yet she needed to ask. "Wyatt, just tell me one thing. You're not married, are you?"

He stared into her eyes for a beat of a second and then shook his head. "No, I can promise you that."

Relief took on a new meaning with that promise. "Then, as much as I like looking at you, I'd like to touch, too."

He sighed, perhaps equally relieved. "Absolutely, darlin'."

The first time Wyatt made love to her, it was an exploration of newness. They were careful with each other as she learned what he liked, while he provided what she wanted. There was heat and pleasure and a development of trust. She did trust Wyatt. She knew he wouldn't abuse her in any way; he was far too much of a gentleman for that. But now, after a short respite, Wyatt was pulling her atop him, kissing her senseless again, and this time both of their guards were down.

"I want you again." The urgent plea tore from his throat.

"I'm here," she whispered, climbing up his body and giving him access to her breasts.

"I'm glad you are," he said, tickling her nipple with the tip of his tongue. Both peaks pebbled up immediately, and wild stirrings began at the apex of her thighs.

Wyatt was the best lover she'd ever had. He could take her from zero to ninety with just a heated look or a bold caress. And he was doing just that with exquisite strokes of his tongue on her breast, the full circle of his mouth drawing her out, making every nerve ending ping and jump.

When he was through making her squirm in delight, he moved down her body, his hand gliding past her waist and his fingers tucking into her sensitive folds. He knew exactly how to caress her. He knew where she needed to be stroked and oh, he was merciless. She cried out, the pleasure so exquisite it was almost painful. Electric sensations rocked her back and forth until she could barely take it another second.

"Kiss me," he ordered, and she obeyed.

And just as their tongues met, her body splintered apart, the amazing orgasm rocketing through her body with enough force to jerk her off the bed. She came down panting, the effects of her release almost mystifying her until she opened her eyes and saw Wyatt staring at her, his darkened gaze hot as fired metal.

He rolled her over onto her back and lifted her hips, positioning her. And then he was inside her again, this time without hesitation. He began thrusting, his erection hard and thick, pulsing with new life. He moved deeper and harder and brought her to the brink of insanity once more. "Come with me this time," he rasped, his throat thick.

And they moved together, arching, aching, a beautiful joining of bodies in complete sync with each other. And when she was primed and eager and staring into his eyes, he tipped his head in acknowledgment. He knew she was ready. Then they rose up and bucked and cried out, her sighs meeting his groans. Her body shattered, just as his came apart.

It was glorious.

She was in heaven.

And she stayed up there awhile before slowly easing down.

Her limbs were weightless now. She felt like a sated rag doll, too limp to move. Wyatt scooped her up in his strong arms and surrounded her with his hot, perfect body. He kissed her cheeks, wove his fingers through her hair.

"Brooke," he whispered over her lips.

"Mmm." She'd never been happier. Or more tired.

"Sleep, darlin'."

"Sorry, can't help it."

"It's okay," he said.

Wrapped up in his arms, she closed her eyes.

Wyatt opened his eyes to a dawn that had long ago broken through the shuttered windows of Brooke's hotel room, streaming bright light inside. The digital clock read eight o'clock and he cursed silently as he untangled himself carefully from Brooke. His heart thumped in his chest as he glanced down at her, looking so peaceful, her eyes closed, that mane of raven hair falling down her back. His body strummed to life again, but he had no time to indulge or to say goodbye to Brooke. No time to look into those pretty brown eyes or hear the sultry tone of her voice.

He should've been on the road an hour ago. He was late, and he'd made Henrietta a promise. He couldn't take advantage of her good nature. Weekends were precious to her.

"Dammit," he muttered as he scrambled to step into his clothes. He hated leaving this way. There was a reason widowers shouldn't have one-night stands. He was out of his element here. He had seconds to make a decision and God only knew if it was the right one, but time was wasting. He scribbled a note to Brooke and left it on the nightstand.

He had nothing to offer Brooke. He was still in love with Madelyn and he had no room for another woman in his life. Not that Brooke seemed to want anything but this one night together. She hadn't asked him a bunch of questions the way women tended to do, and she hadn't hinted at anything more. She was vacationing in Texas and had a life and a business on the West Coast.

The thoughts crowded his mind as he gave her one last glance.

He'd be forever grateful to her for this night. Brooke

had helped him get through a tough day and they'd had a good time.

Actually, they'd had *multiple* good times during the evening.

End of story.

He walked to the door, not surprised by the regret burning a hole in his stomach. He didn't usually walk out on women. But he couldn't stay, either. It was better this way. For her. For both of them.

He turned the doorknob and strode out of the room, leaving Brooke and the Inn at Sweetwater behind.

More than an hour later he'd reached the gates of Blue Horizon Ranch. He was home, back where he belonged. But he'd thought about Brooke most of the way and he'd cursed his best friend, Johnny Wilde, for practically daring him to go to the wedding. Now he had guilt. And memories he couldn't wash from his mind.

Was he a fool to think he was betraying his late wife by enjoying himself with another woman? Johnny would certainly think so. But then, what did he know? He'd been with too many women to count and he'd never found the right one, while Wyatt had met the love of his life and had married her. For that short time—only five years—they'd had together, he'd been happier than he thought possible.

And now he had his precious twins to think about.

He parked the car in front of the house and gave it a quick glance, just as a wave of pain jabbed his gut. He'd never quite gotten over the fact that Madelyn wouldn't be here, greeting him after a trip. That her birthday had come and gone yesterday and there would be no more sweet kisses between them, no emerald sparks of joy in her eyes when he surprised her with a gift. "Sorry, Maddy."

That day nine months ago had ripped his gut in two. Seeing the sheriff at his front door, hat in hand, his face solemn. *Madelyn's had an accident. I'm sorry, Mr. Brandt.*

Wyatt shook off the memory. He had to get his ass inside the house. Henrietta's youngest niece was coming to help him with the twins, so Henrietta could spend the weekend camping in their fifth wheel camper up at the river. Ralph, her husband, wasn't a patient man. He'd been pressing her to retire, and she'd promised him she would as soon as Wyatt found a suitable nanny for the twins. Henrietta was as loyal as they came, and she was good with his kids, but she was exhausted lately. He'd catch her rubbing at her back and taking short naps in those rare times when the twins were both asleep. She'd been here since his folks lived at the ranch, and she was more like family than the help. Clearly, she didn't want to leave Wyatt in the lurch without someone he trusted to care for his children, but the search wasn't going well.

He entered his house and stood in the foyer, listening for baby sounds. "I'm home," he said quietly, just in case Brett and Brianna were napping. And then he heard their voices coming from the great room, which substituted now as a giant playroom, and strode in that direction. His heart warmed immediately when he spotted his kids. The twins were toddling around on the floor, paying Carly no mind as she read them their favorite book, *Goodnight Moon.*

"Hi, Carly," he said to the teenager.

"Oh, hi," she said, glancing at him through her black-rimmed glasses.

At the sound of his voice, Brett, who was scooting a Lego truck along the hardwood floor, and Brianna, who was clutching her doll, abandoned their toys, flapped their arms excitedly and toddled over to him, their smiles lighting him up inside. He scooped both twins up in his arms. "Hello, my babies."

He gave each a kiss on the cheek.

Brianna was more vocal than little Brett. "Daddy! Home. Daddy kisses."

Brett stared at his sister first and then hugged Wyatt around the neck. Nothing was sweeter. Nothing helped his healing more than their unconditional love. He was constantly enveloped in sadness thinking that Madelyn would never know her children. And that his twins had been cheated out of a wonderful mother.

Henrietta walked into the room. Her sturdy build and cinnamon red hair piled in a tight bun atop her head gave her the appearance of a stern woman, but nothing was further from the truth. She was an old softy at heart. "Sorry I'm late," he said, feeling like a heel.

"Not a problem, Wyatt. I hope you had a nice time at the wedding."

An image of Brooke Johnson, naked and asleep in the bed he'd just left, popped into his head. "I did. It was good to see Blake again."

"That's nice. My Ralph is on his way. Carly's been here, playing with the kids. She'll help with feeding them later, and getting them down for their naps. I've got the weekend's meals ready for you in the fridge."

"Thanks, Etta."

Carly stood, picking up a few toys from the floor as she rose. "I can stay overnight if you need me to, Mr. Brandt."

"Thanks, Carly. Let's see how the day goes. I might just need you to come back tomorrow, if you can."

"I can do that, too," she said.

"Okay, great." Wyatt set the kids down and squatted onto the floor next to them. It was a tough balancing act, being in charge of a huge ranch corporation and being Daddy to his children. But he couldn't let them down. They needed the stability of having him here most of the time, knowing that they came first, no matter what.

After Madelyn's death, he'd relied heavily on Henrietta

for support with the kids. But if he didn't find a suitable nanny soon, old Ralph would march in here one day and threaten to knock his block off...with a shotgun.

He had three interviews with potential nannies later this week.

He could only hope.

Three

Brooke
You'll never know how much last night meant to me.
If you ever need me for anything, you can find me at
the Blue Horizon Ranch. Thank you.
Wyatt

Brooke sat on her bed in the guest room of Zane Williams's brand-new gorgeous ranch estate and reread the note for the tenth time this month. She hadn't been able to toss it away. The paper was crumpled and creased, but the words rang out loud and clear. Wyatt had blown her off.

The morning after the wedding, when she'd woken up alone at the inn, she'd read his words and been baffled. She'd been certain Wyatt wasn't the love-'em-and-leave-'em type. She'd been certain they'd wake up together and exchange phone numbers, at the very least. Maybe have breakfast together. Their connection had been powerful, so strong, in fact, it sort of scared her. She'd been sure it wasn't one-sided. Had her BS meter gone on the fritz?

After what Royce Brisbane did to her, she'd turned on her protective radar with all shields up. She'd come to Texas partly to forget about men and romance. And then Wyatt appeared, seemingly out of the blue, and gave her one miraculous day...and night.

Maybe that's all there'd ever be for her, snippets of passion, spread out here and there, but nothing real, nothing permanent. Oddly enough, it was the "thank you" at the end of the note that pissed her off more than anything. As if she'd done him a service.

If you ever need me for anything, you can find me at the Blue Horizon Ranch.

Hell, yeah, she needed him. But right now, her pride interfered with good judgment. Tears entered her eyes. Tears she didn't want. Tears that embarrassed her. She wasn't a teary-eyed romantic fool, but her hormones were out of whack and had been pretty much since she'd missed her last period.

She knew what it meant. She'd taken the test yesterday. She was going to have Wyatt's baby—a result of too much passion and not enough good sense.

She'd slept on the news last night, hoping when she woke up today it would've all gone away, like a bad dream you eventually forget. She hadn't told a soul, but Emma was raising her eyebrows at her lately, asking her why she was tired and looking pale. She blamed it on the Texas heat and humidity. She wasn't used to the sweltering temperatures, but Emma was five months pregnant and having just gone through these early months, she knew the signs all too well.

Dylan popped his head into her room. "Are you gonna come out to the set today, sis?"

"Oh, I don't think so. But thanks."

"What are you gonna do? Stay alone here all day?"

Zane and his new wife, Jessica, had graciously offered for the three of them to stay as his houseguests in the glorious new home Adam Chase had designed as a wedding present, while Dylan shot a Western movie here. Zane had been a neighbor for a time back in Moonlight Beach, California, and Dylan, Zane and Adam were all good friends now. But newlyweds Zane and Jessica were inseparable, and a few days back, they'd left on Zane's spectacular tour bus, heading toward New Orleans to do a round of country music concerts.

Now Dylan, Emma and Brooke had the house all to themselves for the next few weeks.

Emma barged into the room, her growing belly covered by a breezy floral handkerchief dress. "No, she's not spending the day alone. She's going to help me pick out baby girl clothes!"

Brooke forgot about her own problems and jumped up. "You're having a girl?"

Emma nodded, her laughter infectious. She lifted the pointed hem of her dress with both hands, and danced around the room singing, "Yes, yes, we're having a baby girl."

Brooke caught her midstride and hugged her tight. "Oh, this is wonderful. Boy or girl, it doesn't matter, but now we know!"

She peered over Emma's shoulder at her brother. His eyes were gleaming with love for his wife and new child. One would never know the child Emma carried wasn't his. But he loved both mother and child with all of his heart. And that's all that mattered.

Brooke stepped away from Emma and with arms reaching up, walked over to Dylan to give him a giant warm hug. Her big brother was happier than she'd ever seen him. "Congratulations."

Dylan kissed her forehead. "Thanks. We're excited."

"You're going to be outnumbered, you know, with all these women around."

"He's used to it," Emma said, her eyes sparkling with mischief.

"That's right, the big mega movie star has women falling at his feet," Brooke said.

"Not anymore. They know I'm taken." Dylan went to Emma and took her hand. She smiled and then both of them looked Brooke's way. "So, you'll drop by the set with Emma later?" he asked.

"Sure, we'll come by and see you."

She couldn't burst his bubble. She'd been a downer lately, and hadn't been able to concentrate on having a good time. They sensed something was up with her, but hadn't pried. Not yet, anyway. She didn't want to raise any more suspicion. She was having enough trouble accepting the fact that Emma wouldn't be the only new mother around here. And she had no clue of how or when to tell Wyatt Brandt he was going to be a father.

Wyatt sat upon a black gelding with white socks named Oreo and faced the rushing waters of the Willow Springs River. Twenty miles north of Beckon and even farther from his ranch, he was doing Johnny a favor today by coming here. Aside from Johnny Wilde, no one else in the area had as much commonsense knowledge about horseflesh and cattle as Wyatt did. Not that he'd wanted this job. Hell, he was no consultant, but his friend had called him in a panic. Johnny had come down with the flu, hopefully just the twenty-four-hour kind, and he'd needed a replacement, pronto. "You're the only one I trust to do the job," he'd said.

It wasn't the plea, but the weakness in Johnny's voice that had Wyatt agreeing to haul his butt away from Blue Horizon Ranch and his kids today.

He glanced at the men milling around, decked out in fringed leather chaps, Stetsons and snakeskin boots. Actors.

Dressing room trailers—honey wagons, Johnny had called them—were set up in the outlying area and a crew of about fifty were pulling wires, setting up cameras and shouting orders. He'd already spoken with the director today about the scene they were to shoot along the river's edge. The horses and cattle would be crossing in shallow waters, but it was a key concern that no animals or actors be hurt in the highly technical shot.

From a distance, he spotted the star of the movie, Dylan McKay, stepping out of his trailer decked out in a chambray shirt, jeans and a red paisley kerchief around his neck. And then Wyatt froze. He blinked and refocused.

Yep, he wasn't imagining it. Dylan was with a woman. It was *her*.

Brooke Johnson.

What was she doing here? She looked awfully chummy with Dylan, laughing at something he'd said and walking along with him as though she was accustomed to being close to the mega superstar.

Seeing her again sent blazing fireworks off in Wyatt's head. "Uh, Tony?" He took his eyes off Brooke for a second to get the assistant wrangler's attention. "Do you know who that woman is walking with Dylan McKay?" He pointed. "Is her name Brooke Johnson?"

The wrangler scrubbed his jaw, his eyes narrowing a bit to gain a good look. "It's Brooke all right. All the single guys on the crew have been eyeing her. But her name's not Johnson. That's Mr. McKay's sister, Brooke McKay."

"She's Dylan McKay's sister?"

"Yep, that's what they tell me. She's a looker, but she's not the friendly type, if you know what I mean."

No, he didn't know what Tony meant. A knot formed

in the pit of his stomach. The woman he'd met on the road had been friendly and fun and sassy. He'd never describe Brooke as unfriendly. But then, he hadn't known the real Brooke, had he? She'd given him a fake name. Now that wasn't cool.

And just like that, Brooke turned her head and met his gaze. She halted abruptly, her face going as white as newly plowed snow. Dylan kept walking, but Brooke stood there, some twenty feet away, staring at him as if she couldn't believe it. As if she wanted to hide under a rock.

God, when had his effect on women taken a turn for the worse?

She said something to her brother, and then did a one-eighty and hightailed it back to the trailer. Before stepping inside she glanced in Wyatt's direction. To see if he was watching? Their eyes met again and for all he was worth, he couldn't, wouldn't stop looking at her. Then she was gone, the trailer door slamming shut behind her.

"Crap," he muttered, climbing down from his horse. He planted his feet on solid ground and held the reins in his hand, trying to decide what to do. He'd worked hard to put Brooke out of his mind, and now here she was infiltrating, invading and trying her best to take up space again.

He was so busy being in his own head, he didn't notice Dylan McKay until he was standing right in front of him. "Hello, I'm Dylan. I understand you're taking over for Johnny Wilde today?"

"Yes," Wyatt said, distracted. He got it together enough to refocus and pay the star some attention. "Wyatt Brandt."

Dylan put out his hand. "Nice meeting you."

"Same here."

They shook hands. "I understand you think the river's too fast to do the crossing scene today?"

"That's right. I told the director we should wait. I know the area, and that current is only going to get stronger as the day progresses. It's not safe for the animals. Clouds are starting to gather and those breezes are gonna turn ugly in a few hours. The winds will only complicate things. Sorry, I know it's not the news you hoped to hear."

"No need to apologize. We can shoot around it. Keeping the animals and crew safe is a priority. I just wanted to hear it from you."

"Sure thing."

"So, you're from around here?"

"I've lived in Texas all my life. I own Blue Horizon Ranch some twenty-five miles from here."

"Horses?"

"Cattle, but we have a string of Arabians and cutting horses on the ranch, too."

They spoke about horses and Texas for a while, and Wyatt came away thinking that Dylan McKay wasn't a stereotypical prima donna celebrity. It was on the tip of his tongue during the conversation to ask him about Brooke. But that didn't happen. Dylan had been called away. Just as well. Wyatt had come to the conclusion that he needed to speak to Brooke himself.

Sure, she'd lied to him about who she was.

But he'd left her alone in a hotel room after a wild night of sex, without much of an explanation.

He marched over to the honey wagon with a clear vision of what needed saying, but as he came close to knocking on the trailer door, his mind began to blur. Visions of Brooke slapping his face a good one flashed in his head. She might call security to toss him off the property.

He'd like to see them try.

But his hand clenched into a fist and he rapped on the door regardless. Things needed saying. It was as simple as that.

The door opened, and he was shell-shocked when a

pretty, pregnant redhead stood facing him. "Hi, can I help you?"

"Uh, sure. I wanted to speak with Brooke. I'm Wyatt Brandt."

"Okay, Wyatt. Let me see if Brooke is available. What can I tell her this is about?"

Hell, the wagon wasn't that big. Brooke was probably hearing this whole conversation. "Just mention my name. Tell her I hope she'll see me."

"I'll see him, Emma." Brooke said, her voice stony. And then she appeared in the doorway. She wasn't happy about seeing him, yet her beautiful brown eyes widened a bit when she looked at him, turning his brain to mush. The words he wanted to say fled him faster than a jack-rabbit running from a hound.

"Hello, Brooke."

"Wyatt."

Emma gave them both a curious glance. "You know, I just remembered I have an errand to run."

Out here? There wasn't a town for miles.

"You don't have to leave, Emma. This won't take long," Brooke told her.

"No, no. I've really got to, to, uh…talk to Dylan. He's waiting on me to meet him down by the river."

Emma ducked her head and scooted down the steps quickly, giving them privacy.

Brooke's curvy body blocked the doorway. "I'm not inviting you in."

"There's no need for that. I just wanted to say…" Brooke's arms were folded and any minute now, she'd be tapping her foot, schoolteacher style. "Listen, I have some explaining to do. But so do you. You lied to me."

"About what?"

"About your name. You faked your identity."

"I have my reasons for that. But you skipped out...and oh, never mind."

"Can we talk?"

"I thought that's what we're doing."

"No, I mean really talk. I feel badly about how I had to leave you that morning. I do, and I want to make it up to you."

If body language had anything to do with it, she'd surely refuse him, but something stopped her. Instead, she seemed to be considering it. "What did you have in mind?"

"Come out to the ranch and have dinner with me. We can talk there, uninterrupted." Well, that depended on two little rascals and their sleep schedule, but he couldn't offer her anything more right now. His sense of honor was at stake. He didn't usually treat women the way he'd treated Brooke, and he wanted to make amends. "I can pick you up later and take you to the ranch."

"No. I don't think so," she said, and he felt the disappointment all the way to his toes. "I'll drive out. Just give me directions...*easy directions*, or I may not find it," she said.

She was agreeing? Why was he so damn happy about that?

"Great. It's about half an hour's drive from here and it's practically a straight run. I'll write down the directions. But I'd be happy to pick you up."

"No, I'll drive to you," she said, in a tone that meant business.

He got it. She wanted to be able to leave at a moment's notice. He didn't care. At least the nagging thoughts plaguing his mind would be put to rest after he explained the whole one-night-stand business.

The trick was trying to sort it all out in his own head first.

With her windows rolled down and a light drizzle dotting her windshield, Brooke was actually enjoying the ride.

The muggy Texas day had given way to an evening of fresh scents and cooler temperatures. Her windshield wipers clicked on and off and her driving arm was hit with an occasional raindrop as she steered over remote terrain toward Wyatt Brandt's ranch.

If it weren't for the baby she was carrying, she wouldn't be making this drive, but the opportunity to tell Wyatt the truth presented itself today when he shown up on the set of *The Price of Glory*. Seeing pigs fly would've shocked her less than having Wyatt Brandt appear at the river.

But as luck or bad karma would have it—she wasn't sure which—Wyatt had come out of nowhere again, her not-so-miraculous cowboy. Talking to him had become inevitable. She certainly couldn't speak with him on Dylan's set; there were too many opportunities to trigger gossip and speculation. And at Zane's home, there'd be too many eyes and ears around to have a private conversation, namely her brother's and Emma's.

Country music filled the silence of the road. Brooke sang along with Reba to keep her mind off what she was about to do. The words of "Cowgirls Don't Cry" poured out of her as she traveled over a lovely wooden bridge, the creek below surging with water. Alongside the water's edge, a carpet of healthy bluebonnets stretched out as far as the eye could see.

The picturesque image stayed with her and gave her a sense of peace. Soon white fences lined with Mexican oaks standing tall and probably designed for privacy came into view. Long branches with leathery leaves waved at her as she drove by. Within a minute, she came upon brick columns and iron gates and a pretty metal sign embossed with the sun rising over the land, welcoming her to Blue Horizon Ranch.

She sighed. Grateful to have made it without getting lost or running out of gas, she now had to contend with the fact that she was *here*. And one way or another, her life was going to change forever when she revealed her pregnancy to Wyatt Brandt.

As she drove through the open gates, the sudden strong scent of cattle filled her nostrils. Texans told her she'd get used to the smells around these parts, but it wasn't exactly vanilla sugar she was breathing in and she sincerely doubted that smell would be a treat to her nose anytime soon.

But oh man, the ranch was beautiful. The branches of whispering oaks formed a canopy over the road leading to a beautiful slate-gray stone ranch house. Wide windows gave the place an open feel. Across the way, the barns and outer buildings were faced with white wood and gray-toned shutters. It was homey and contemporary at the same time. Brooke immediately loved Wyatt's home. From the outside.

What lay in store for her on the inside was another matter.

She drove the circular drive and parked the car. She was on time for a change.

She'd dressed for dinner in old Brooke style, wearing basic black hip-hugging slacks, a silver-and-black shimmery top, and a wide belt. Her shoes were skyscrapers in red suede. She wasn't entirely sure she'd dressed this way out of defiance or as a shield of armor. She knew one thing: she felt comfortable in her own skin, and right now she needed that burst of confidence to confront Wyatt and tell him the truth.

She knocked at the door, and when nothing happened, she hit the doorbell. Inside, she heard the chimes ring out. A moment later, the door opened and she stood face-to-face with Wyatt.

Holding a squirming baby boy dressed in tiny denim overalls.

It was the last thing she expected. The child's melt-your-heart blue eyes were a perfect match to Wyatt's. The baby took one look at her and turned his head into Wyatt's shoulder and clung on for dear life.

"Wyatt?" She was rendered speechless after that, staring at the man who'd made her insides quiver just one month ago. Now he looked the picture of domesticity, his pale blue shirtsleeves rolled up, a stain that looked like sweet potato on his collar, his short blond hair disheveled.

"Come in, Brooke. I'm glad you made it okay."

She stared at him, still not believing what she was seeing. He'd never mentioned having a child. Although there'd seemed to be a silent agreement between them not to delve too deeply into their private lives. But being a father? Having a child was news he should've shared with her.

When she stood rooted to the spot, Wyatt moved aside and nodded, encouraging her to enter the house.

She stepped inside, instantly aware of her surroundings: the planks of light gray flooring under her feet, the brightness of the rooms even as dusk was settling. But what struck her the most was seeing the parlor crowded with toys: a fire truck and princess car suitable for a toddler and musical instruments and blocks everywhere. Everything was tidy and yet, it was *there*.

Wyatt closed the door behind her. "This is Brett, my son. He was supposed to be sleeping by the time you arrived. Obviously that didn't happen. Babies tend to make liars of their parents."

"You never mentioned you had a child, Wyatt." She tried hard not to put accusation in her tone.

"Would that have made a difference?"

"I don't know." It was the truth. She'd been so incredibly drawn to Wyatt that if he'd been open with her and told her he was a father, would she have fallen so easily into bed with him? She wasn't sure.

The baby inclined his head toward her, his rosy face so sweet, so curious. "Hello, Brett."

Brett clung tighter to Wyatt's neck.

"He's not much of a talker yet."

"How old is he?"

"Going on nineteen months."

"He's beautiful, Wyatt."

"Thanks, he's the best part of me. Well, him and his twin sister, Brianna."

"There's two of them?" Her ears twitched at the sound of her own voice. Twins? Wyatt had two children. This was all a bit much for her to take in. Her crazy hormones brought the threat of tears. She forced them down and tried not to think about what his reaction would be when she told him her news.

"Yes, and they're a handful, believe me. Listen, I want to explain all this to you. Why don't you have a seat in the dining room?" He started walking and she followed. "There's wine and cheese and other snacks ready. My housekeeper, Henrietta, is gone for the day, but she put out a nice spread for us. It'll just take me a few minutes to put Brett down to sleep and change my clothes."

He gave her another cursory glance. "You look pretty, by the way," he said, his miracle cowboy charm taking hold again. He was such a freaking gentleman, she had trouble remembering how he'd dumped her after a spectacular night of sex.

A night that they'd conceived a child.

"Please," he was saying, "have a seat."

Robotically she obeyed. And once he excused himself, she sat there stunned and feeling foolish. Her perfect miracle cowboy had engaged in lies of omission. Was he at that wedding just to hook up with a woman? Was her man radar off that much that she couldn't recognize a player?

But deep inside, she kept telling herself it wasn't true.

She couldn't have been that much off the mark with Wyatt. He'd been wonderful that night, and today, he'd invited her to his ranch to explain. Yet it nagged at her that if they hadn't accidentally met today, it would've been solely up to her to seek him out. It put her in an awkward spot.

A waterfall of rain poured over the gutter above the dining room bay window, drawing her attention. Lit by surrounding lights, it was a pretty distraction even if the skies were dark and filled with dreary clouds. It sort of mirrored her mood right now. Her nerves were jumping, and she bounded up to walk around the room, stopping to look at the pretty things in the china hutch, expensive yet tasteful pieces of crystal, delicate dishes and gold-rimmed teacups.

"That teacup set dates back to post-Civil War," Wyatt said quietly.

She hadn't heard him enter the room, but he stood behind her now and when she turned around, he was a breath away, staring into her eyes. The faint hint of his cologne brought reminders of being naked with him, of his hands on her and...

"It was my grandmother's favorite..." His voice trailed off as his gaze dipped down to her mouth.

Brooke felt the jolt down to her toes and looked away, pretending interest in the rain.

She wasn't going there with him, not again. There was too much unsaid between them.

He sighed and stepped away, pulling out a chair for her. The table was set perfectly, with some of the same fine china from the cabinet. She sat back down. Before he took a seat, he offered her a glass of wine.

"No thanks," she said. No alcohol for her.

He nodded, probably thinking she was being careful because she'd have to drive home. Well, there was that, too.

"You haven't touched anything," he noted.

"I'm not hungry right now, Wyatt." She was queasy about being here and queasy in general due to being pregnant.

"Okay, we can wait on dinner."

He braced his elbows on the table, matched the fingers of both hands in a steeple under his chin and sighed. "Brooke, I'm very glad you're here. The way I left you that morning was...unforgivable. I was out of my element and unsure what to do."

"You didn't appear unsure of anything the night we were together."

"Maybe it was you..."

"Don't butter me up, Wyatt. I can't get past the fact that if we hadn't accidentally met today, I would've never heard from you."

"You gave me a fake name."

"And you ran out on me after we..." She shook off the thought. She'd been over this in her mind a hundred times.

"I guess we both have explaining to do."

"You go first," she said. "And then I'll let you know if I want to share my reasons with you."

He nodded. Of the two sins, his was by far the worst, and he seemed to know it by the miserable look on his face. "My explanation is simple, but hard to admit. I lost my wife about ten months ago. She got in the car one day to pick up diapers for the twins and she never returned. She was pushed off the road by a semitruck. Her car plummeted off the shoulder and crashed into a tree."

Brooke gasped quietly, surprised to learn of Wyatt's loss. It explained a lot about why he hadn't spoken much about his past. He was probably still in a great deal of pain. When she'd met him he'd told her he was newly single. She'd thought that meant he had broken up with a girlfriend, or he was divorced. It never occurred to her that he might be a widower.

"That's awful, Wyatt. I'm so incredibly sorry."

She couldn't imagine losing someone she loved that way. One minute they were alive and vital and then in the blink of an eye, they're gone. How terribly sad it was for the mother who would never know her children. And those poor little babies, too. It was tragic all the way around.

She'd never forget how she felt when Dylan's life was in danger. She'd been absolutely terrified for him and she couldn't imagine losing him. But Wyatt had had to face that reality. He'd become a widower at a very young age.

"Thanks. I've been wallowing in self-pity and grief and as you can see, I have my hands full with the twins. They're about all I can handle. Two is like having four. Henrietta keeps reminding me how hard it is on her. I'm trying my best to find a suitable nanny, but it isn't easy. The last two who worked for me were mediocre at best. The babies didn't seem to respond to them, and they flaked on us a few times. I can't have that. I need someone reliable. Henrietta is sticking with me for the short term. She's getting on in age and she just can't do both jobs. I offered to hire more help so she could take the kids on full-time, but her hubby is chomping at the bit for her to retire. I can't say as I blame him."

Wyatt's shoulders lifted in a shrug that spoke volumes about his frustration. "My friend Johnny Wilde pressed me to go to that wedding. He said I had to get out and start living my life again. So, between him and Henrietta urging me on, I decided to go. The wedding was a way to distract me from the real issue that day. It was Madelyn's birthday. She would've been thirty."

Brooke was beginning to get the picture. "Was *I* your distraction, Wyatt?"

He gazed into her eyes, and his head made a slight movement. Was that a yes or a no? She couldn't tell what he was thinking or what he was about to say by the sol-

emn expression on his face. "You were...but in an unexpected way."

"What does that mean?" She found herself speaking
quietly, and not because of the sleeping children. This was
delicate subject matter and Wyatt was looking so miserable.

"I thought I'd attend the nuptials, wish Blake well and
bide my time during the reception. There'd be some drown-
ing of my sorrows in whiskey, too, and then I'd planned
on turning in early. I didn't go there with anything else
in mind. I couldn't stop thinking about Madelyn and how
we would've spent the day celebrating her birthday together. But then I found you broken down on the road,
and I couldn't drive on by. I stopped and well, that's the
unexpected part. For the first time since Madelyn died, I
started enjoying myself again. Just being in your company
changed my outlook and made me glad I'd made the trip
to the inn. You made me forget some pretty awful days
and I...well damn, this isn't easy to admit."

He pushed his fingers through his hair and sighed from
deep in his chest. "I was attracted to you, Brooke. Madelyn was my whole life and I can't even remember a time
that I wasn't infatuated with her. But then I had this one
day with you."

"So I was a hall pass from your grief and guilt?"

He nodded. "Sounds awful, but maybe that's exactly
how it was."

"So you woke up the next day and ran...because the
guilt came back? You couldn't face me? Why didn't you
wake me or at least wait until we could say goodbye?"

Wyatt reached across the wide table and touched her
fingers, as if he needed the connection with her. Sparks
ran up her arm, but she wouldn't make anything out of it.
Wyatt was clearly still in love with his wife.

"No, Brooke. It wasn't that. It was Henrietta. She'd

stayed overnight with the babies, and I'd promised her I'd be back early in the morning. She had a trip planned and I didn't want to ruin her day or abuse her good nature. I woke up later than expected that morning. Believe me, there was so much I wanted to say to you. But that note was all I had time for, and that's the honest truth. On my babies' lives, I swear to you."

Brooke was quiet for a time. He was giving her time to absorb it all. She took a swallow of her drink and began nodding her head. "Okay, I get that. But you know what part of the note insulted me more than anything? The thank-you at the end."

Wyatt stared at her and shook his head. "You're mad because I thanked you?"

"It was as if…as if I'd done a service for you or something. I can't explain it, but that's how I felt when I woke up alone and found your thank-you note."

"Oh, man." He rubbed his forehead and closed his eyes. "I had no idea it would come off that way. I wasn't proud of how I left that day. It's bothered me all this time. Believe me, Brooke, I never intended to hurt you."

Thunder boomed off in the distance and she jumped. Was it a heavenly omen, a sign to take Wyatt at his word?

"I'm out of practice with women, Brooke. And I never expected to have…"

"Sex?"

He nodded. It wasn't in his wheelhouse to be crude; she'd already figured that out about him. But she had no problem telling it like it is.

"It was an amazing night, Brooke. But I didn't think past that night or what the next day would bring."

"I didn't either, if I'm being honest."

"But you didn't expect me to run out on you."

She nodded. "It made what could've been a good memory for me feel cheap."

"No!" Wyatt scraped his chair back and stood. "No, Brooke. That night…it was real and honest. I needed to feel alive again…and it was you, and only you, who helped me with that. And if I'm not mistaken, you needed the same from me, too. Am I right?"

She opened her mouth, but her denial didn't come. Slowly, she closed her trap and nodded. She would give Wyatt that. She'd needed someone who'd cared—if only in the moment—for her. She was still healing from Royce's duplicity. She would've almost rather had her ex throw her over for another woman than to use her the way he had.

Wyatt was a different breed of man. That much she knew. "You didn't tell me you had children."

"I didn't. I just wanted to be me, not a father, not a widower, that night. My pain-in-the-ass pal Johnny is forever saying I need to find myself again. That's what I was trying to do."

She inhaled a sharp breath, everything becoming clear in her mind now. He was lost without his wife.

A flash of lightning lit up the night sky behind Wyatt and reflected off the window. The bright beam illuminated a backyard filled with patio tables and chairs, toys and a gated pool. This was a home for a family to live and love and thrive in, but sadly there was a missing piece now. The family wasn't whole anymore.

Her anger faded as fast as the lightning. Oddly, she understood how Wyatt wanted to be private about his past when they'd met, wanting one night to just be himself and not a responsible father, not a grieving widower. Wasn't that the same reason she hadn't been totally honest with him? She just wanted to be Brooke, not Dylan McKay's younger sister, not the girl who'd had men use her to get close to her famous brother.

If she were brave, she'd reveal her pregnancy to Wyatt and try to cope with the decisions they would make together. But her courage failed her. She couldn't lay this on Wyatt right now.

As she grappled with her decision to cut and run, a baby's wail broke into her thoughts, loud and panicky.

Wyatt's squeezed his eyes shut momentarily. "That's Brianna. Sorry. I think she's having a bad dream. I've got to check on her. "

"Of course. Go."

As soon as Wyatt took a step out of the dining room, another howl erupted, the second one huskier and deeper than the first. Both babies had woken up. And their cries blasted through the house without interval. Double trouble. Brooke rose and followed Wyatt up the stairs.

At least this was one crisis she could help manage.

Four

Brett and Brianna both howled, one in each crib, their little bodies facing up toward glow-in-the-dark neon stars illuminating the ceiling. Madelyn had chosen nursery decor that would bring a sense of peace and calm, but there were times that nothing much soothed cranky twins. Thunder boomed outside, rattling the windows, and their cries grew louder. Wyatt picked up Brett first, bouncing him in his arms, and then turned to Brianna. But Brooke was already picking up his little girl.

Brianna was groggy at best, her eyes half closed. But she looked so sweet, her blond curls falling onto her face as she clung to Brooke's neck. She had no clue she was in the arms of a stranger. Heaven help them all when she discovered that fact. Bri was his wild child. She didn't take to newcomers, which was something her previous nannies had learned the hard way.

Brooke bounced Brianna in her arms, taking her cue from him. Not that he knew exactly what he was doing.

His kids were a constant bafflement to him. One minute they were happy as clams, the next, they'd be wailing about something he couldn't begin to fathom.

Bouncing them was clearly not working. Tears continued to fall, and then Brooke began to sing as she rocked the baby in her arms. Not just *sing*: her lilting voice filled the room with sweetness, a serene siren's song that mesmerized with its beauty. And damn if Brianna didn't stop crying right then and there. Her big blue eyes opened wide and she sniffled a few times, stunned into silence by her own curiosity and...awe.

Brett followed suit, and Wyatt walked him closer to Brooke, so he, too, could be enchanted. Brooke clearly had a talent, which seemed to pour out of her effortlessly. Within minutes, his crab apple little ones were quieted. Brooke rocked Bri and he rocked Brett and once they'd fallen asleep in their arms, Wyatt nodded to Brooke. Carefully, she laid the baby down in her crib. Then Wyatt kissed Brett on the forehead and also set him in his crib.

Brooke tiptoed out of the room, allowing Wyatt a minute to simply stare at his babies. God, he loved them. They were all he had left of Madelyn, and they truly were the best part of him. He would do just about anything to ensure their happiness. But with one strike against them already—losing their beautiful mother—the weight of his responsibility sometimes scared the stuffing out of him.

He left the nursery door open and went in search of Brooke. He found her at the top of the stairs, waiting for him. "They're both sweet," she whispered. "You're very lucky."

"Thanks. You have a beautiful voice, Brooke. Hidden talent? Or did you lie to me about your profession?"

Her body went rigid. Fueled by anger, her brown eyes lit up. "I didn't lie to you about anything but my name."

"Yeah, and why was that? You feel like telling me

now?" he asked softly, trying to tread carefully. He'd pissed her off unintentionally, but he really wanted to know.

Her shoulders relaxed some, and she studied him a moment, then nodded. "All right. I'll explain."

"Great. Let's talk downstairs." He took her arm and led her to the parlor sofa. "Have a seat."

She sat on the couch and he took a seat on the opposite end.

"It's not a big deal," she began, "that I lied about my last name. My brother is famous and it gets old real fast, having people act nice to me only because of him."

"That's it? That's why you lied? You get tired of answering questions about him?"

"No, Wyatt. I get tired of men using me, getting my hopes up and pretending to care about me only to get close to *him*. I get tired of men giving me scripts or screenplays to show him or using me to ask him to invest in their pet projects."

Wyatt shook his head, finally getting the picture. It wasn't pretty. It would take a strong, secure woman not to be affected, but then, Brooke was all those things, which made the creeps using her horrible slugs. "You've been burned."

"To a crisp."

"Man, that's rough. I'm sorry. Was it someone in particular, someone special?"

"I thought he was special at the time. It was a man who worked in finance, a real pencil pusher, a numbers man, a guy I thought wouldn't care who my brother was. As it turned out Royce was a closet wannabe screenwriter. And when he lowered the boom I didn't see it coming. It floored me and hurt me, and coming to Texas was a way to mend and heal. And gain some perspective. So, what I did that day by lying to you wasn't too different than what you'd done. I just wanted a day without questions. One day to be me. Just plain Brooke."

"You could never be plain," he said, and realized how much he meant it. From the get-go, he'd found something unique in Brooke.

"Thanks." She shrugged and looked away as if she didn't believe him, as if what he was saying to her was merely a platitude to make her feel better. Yes, he wanted her to feel better, but he wasn't lying.

"It's the truth. And I do understand. I'm sorry you got hurt, Brooke. Honestly, it makes me feel awful about running out on you the way I did."

She snapped off a quick smile. "Story of my life."

"You're terrific, Brooke. I mean that. And any creep who would use you isn't fit to call himself a man."

"Present company excluded?"

"I didn't use you. Tell me you don't think that."

Her eyes squeezed closed and she shook her head. "No. I don't think that. Not anymore."

Which meant she'd gone the entire month thinking he had. Crap.

Wyatt closed the gap between them on the sofa. He had to get closer to her now, and make sure she was okay. Hell, she was more than okay. She was amazing. It wasn't easy being this close without touching her, holding her in his arms and making her feel better. But sanity prevailed just in time and took over his brain. Touching her again would be a colossal mistake. A change of subject was needed.

"You're very good with children. Do you have a big family?"

"Not really. I'm Dylan's foster sister—his folks are my folks. It was just me and him growing up. He's always been my rock, my best friend, and sometimes, my bitter enemy. You know, your usual brother/sister dynamic."

"Sounds like fun."

"Yeah, it was. Still is. I love him to death. What about you? Brothers or sisters?"

"Nope, just me and those two powerhouses you helped put to sleep. They're a handful and a half. I don't know how people with big families do it. One boy, one girl, and I'm done. Especially now."

"You mean because you're doing it without their mother?" Brooke's voice lowered and nearly cracked. She wouldn't look him in the face.

"Two's enough, when both parents are in the picture. But yeah, I suppose it's because I'm trying to move on and it's tough going sometimes. That's why when I met you…well, it was nice. *You* were nice, and I suppose I—"

"Don't, Wyatt. I get the picture."

She went rigid all over and lowered her lids to her red suede shoes. They looked great on her feet, but weren't exactly perfect footwear for a rainy night. "Maybe you don't."

"Oh, believe me, I do." Her voice was stronger now, but pained, as if he'd hurt her all over again.

Just then, lightning flashed, and a second later thunder cracked, the loud boom shaking the house. Wyatt bounded up quickly and moved to the window. Rain was coming down in buckets. This raging storm wasn't moving on anytime soon. "Dammit. I should've been paying closer attention."

"To what?" Brooke asked.

He turned to her while releasing a you're-a-fool sigh aimed at himself. "The rain. The storm. This isn't good, Brooke."

"Won't it pass?" She rose and marched over to the window.

"Not before doing a lot of damage. The bridge is washed out by now. Happens every time we have a major storm."

"What bridge? Not that pretty little bridge I drove over a couple of hours ago?"

"That's the one. It's the only way in and out of the ranch. Can't get to the highway without it. You're going to have to spend the night here."

Her face twisted up, and those chocolate eyes went dark as coal. "That's ridiculous, Wyatt. I. Am. Not. Spending the night here."

"Hey, I know you don't want to, but this storm is dangerous. And you won't get over that bridge. Trust me."

She shook her head. "I'm betting it's not too late. If I leave now, I'll make it. The rain only just started coming down hard."

"Nope, not happening. I can't let you do it."

"You can't order me to stay here." Her voice rose. "I'm going to try, Wyatt."

She found her purse, grabbed her car keys and made a dash for the front door.

He followed her. "Brooke, be reasonable." But the determined look on her face said reason wasn't a factor.

"Thanks for dinner."

"You didn't eat a thing."

"Thanks anyway. I'll…we'll talk. I have to go."

He blocked the door with his arm. "Don't. It's not safe."

It wasn't safe for her to stay overnight either, but he wasn't going there.

She gazed into his eyes. There was something more going on with her. Something that he didn't understand. Was she worried about a repeat of the night they'd shared? He'd hurt her, and she wasn't forgetting that anytime soon, but for some reason he didn't believe that was it. He thought they'd cleared the air. They'd talked openly and honestly, but something had jarred her and he wasn't sure what it was.

"You don't have to worry about, about…"

"Don't be an idiot, Wyatt. You think you're that irresistible?"

She blinked her eyes; her sarcasm was hiding something else. Something she wasn't saying. Having her spend the night here wouldn't be easy on him. He wasn't immune to her, the way she claimed to be to him. She was the only other woman beside Madelyn to touch something deep inside him and bring out his protective instincts. Was it a bad case of lust? He'd gone months without sex, and Brooke had been the perfect partner, guileless and beautiful and giving. Having her here would test his willpower, but the very thought of her going out in that storm gave him hives. She didn't know the roads like he did. She didn't know the treachery that lay in her path. She came from California, where a few sprinkles meant storm watch. But here in Texas, they had real storms, ones that could wipe out entire towns.

"Brooke, listen to me. You're being stubborn."

"And you're wasting my time. You can't keep me here against my will," she hissed out.

Holy hell, she was right. "I am trying to keep you safe."

"I don't need you to rescue me anymore. You're through being my miracle cowboy, Wyatt. Now, unblock the door."

Slowly and against his God-given good judgment, he stepped away from the door.

She exited quickly, and he watched her get into her car, start the engine and pull away.

The windshield wipers weren't doing a very good job. Or was it her tears causing her vision to blur? She slowed the car down to a snail's crawl and inched her way along the dark road leading her away from Wyatt, his kids, his grief and his declaration that he wanted no more children. Period. *Two's enough.* Two, as in his adorable twins who were motherless now, and being raised by a dad who was lost in his own way.

And where did that leave her?

More tears spilled onto her cheeks, mingling with the raindrops that had slashed across her face just minutes ago as she got into her car. Damn her hormones. She was usually stronger than this. But usually, she wasn't pregnant by a virtual stranger whose only sin, other than running out on her in the morning after a one-night stand, was that he had no clue how her heart had shattered and was still shattering when she realized that he wasn't going to jump for joy at having another child.

And dammit, her child deserved more than that. Her child didn't deserve being cast aside. She should know. The McKays had taken her in and loved her like their own. She was grateful every day of her life, but it still didn't heal her secret pain of knowing that she'd been unwanted. Unloved. It was classic foster-child syndrome. But now, her baby, the sweet life growing inside her, wouldn't have what Brooke had vowed any child she bore would have: two loving parents.

"Not fair," she mumbled while trying to slosh along the flooded, muddy road.

A flash of lightning lit up the skies and thunder followed, the loudest she'd ever heard. Her hands trembled on the steering wheel, and she sobered. Maybe Wyatt wasn't trying to be Prince Charming again. Maybe this storm was really as bad as he'd said.

An animal skittered across the road and she braked hard. "Oh!" She barely missed the critter, and the car skidded, careering to the right. She gripped the steering wheel tighter, her knuckles white, as the car spun out of control. The back end dipped into a muddy ditch and hit a brick fence post. The force pitched her forward and her thick skull slammed into the steering wheel.

The jolt startled her, and her forehead immediately throbbed. She sat there, dazed, as big drops of rain pelted the windshield. Her head pounded, her eyes burned and she felt as if she'd been hit by a giant dump truck rather than mixing it up with a fence post. She closed her eyes, a sense of déjà vu hitting her. She'd been in this car once before and laid her head on the steering wheel, clueless as to how to proceed. God, she was an idiot.

Tears sprang anew from her eyes, and she welcomed them this time. She needed a good cry. What secretly pregnant girl didn't?

She took a tissue out of her purse and blew her nose. That's when she realized it wasn't just tears streaking her face. Blood colored the white tissue. Not a lot, but enough for her to take another tissue out and adjust the mirror in the dark to catch a glimpse of the damage. She had a knot the size of a plum erupting and a scrape two inches long. No doubt tomorrow, it would turn from hot red to dark purple. Wonderful. Now she'd have to explain all this to Dylan and Emma and endure their worry and concern.

If she ever got home tonight.

A knock came on the driver's side window, startling her out of her self-pity. Oh, no. It couldn't be. The man wearing a rain slicker and big Western hat gestured for her to roll down her window.

She did. He shone a flashlight on her face and then quickly lowered it. But it must have been enough for him to see her stricken expression and bruised forehead. Curses spilled from his mouth. Really ugly words hissed out, not exactly the words of a knight in shining armor. Lucky for her, the pound of the rain washed away the worst of them from her delicate ears.

"Wyatt."

"Dammit, Brooke. You're bleeding."

"Not that much," she said numbly.

"Are you okay?"

"I… I think so."

He yanked the door open and reached for her.

"I can walk."

"Quiet, Brooke," he said through clenched teeth. There was fierceness in his voice she'd never heard before. So she clamped her trap shut as he lifted her out of the car and carried her to a big four-wheel-drive Jeep. He dumped her in the front seat, but not before her eyes drifted to the backseat. And her stomach plummeted. Two beautiful children, strapped into their car seats wearing pajamas and shivering, were rustling around back there, restless, cold and sleepy-eyed.

Brett rubbed his eyes and Brianna was barely holding back sleep-deprived tears.

Wyatt had risked going out in the storm with his babies to save her sorry butt.

He slammed the door shut behind him and didn't look at her. "I'm…sorry about this, Wyatt."

Nothing.

She bit her lip. His seething anger was almost tangible, and she felt the slap of his silence as he pulled out onto the road and slowly navigated his way through the storm. The rain didn't let up, and the windshield wipers fought a crazy swish and slosh of water. But she felt safe again and knew he would steer them cautiously home. Lights from the ranch house appeared out of the darkness like a beacon of all things good, and Wyatt drove into the attached garage and killed the engine. He would've probably liked to kill her, too, at the moment. Brett had started crying halfway through the drive home and Brianna had joined in shortly after. The cacophony of their cries only added weight to her blunder.

She was a heel.

A thoughtless fool.

She hadn't once thought of the risk to her own baby in all this.

And Wyatt's innocent kids had been dragged through the storm in the dead of night.

Of course, she'd thought of none of this beforehand. She'd only wanted to make a clean getaway. She didn't think she could bear staying the night under Wyatt's roof, and guess what? *Hello.* Now she had no choice in the matter. And instead of Wyatt being a gracious host, she'd be privy to his wrath.

Which she deserved.

Wyatt gave her a cursory look, only to gauge her injuries. "Stay put in the Jeep. I'll be back for you," he ordered.

"You don't need to do that," she said, opening the door and practically falling out. It was a long way down, and she'd been in a hurry. "I'm helping with the kids. You take Brett, I'll get Brianna."

"Brooke," he said, his sigh weary and frustrated, but he didn't argue the point. It was too loud in the garage to hear much beyond the babies' cries.

"Let me help, Wyatt," she said softly. "It's the least I can do."

"You're not dizzy?"

She was dizzy in the brain lately, but that wasn't what Wyatt meant. "No. I'm not. It's just a little bump."

He grunted and she took that as a yes to helping with the kids.

She opened the back door of the Jeep, ignoring the throbbing pain in her head, and concentrated on unfastening Brianna from the car seat. The baby was pushing the heels of her hands into her tired eyes, whimpering. "Come with me, Bri baby. We'll get you warm and back to sleep."

Apparently at some point, Wyatt had tossed two blankets over them, but now they lay on the Jeep's floor. She grabbed one and wrapped it around the baby, while Wyatt was doing his best with Brett. Once they had their two unruly packages all bundled up, they entered the house. Immediate warmth settled around them as they made their way up the stairs.

The nursery was illuminated by a night-light. Brooke and Wyatt stood quietly in the center of the room rocking the babies. Their cries simmered some, but they were still restless.

"Wyatt?" she whispered.

"Hmm?"

"Do you have your cell phone handy?"

"Yeah, why?" he whispered, still swaying little Brett in his arms.

"I need it for a minute."

He gave her a look, but then handed it to her.

"Thanks."

She set Brianna down in her crib and covered her with a blanket. Brooke then fidgeted with the phone until she found what she was looking for. "Okay," she said, "put Brett in his crib."

Wyatt gave her a dubious look, but set the baby down and covered him.

Then she turned up the volume on the phone and the gentle humming of a box fan filled the room.

"They should be asleep in minutes," she whispered to Wyatt.

"What in hell is that?" he asked, staring at her as if she'd grown horns.

"White noise."

She tiptoed out of the room. Wyatt glanced at his quieted babies, not quite asleep yet, but soothed and calmer now, before following behind her.

In the hallway, he grabbed her hand. "Come with me."

His grip was tight, but not in a loving way. She felt a lecture coming on. But to her surprise, he led her into his master bedroom. It was a beautiful room filled with white oak furniture in tasteful shades of cream and lilac. Madelyn's touch was all around, from the top-notch drapes and bed linens to the delicate crystal perfume bottles on the dresser to the impressionist pastel artworks on the wall. It was hardly a manly rancher's room, and Brooke had trouble picturing Wyatt in here. Yet it was a testament to his love for his wife. He'd let her decorate, allowing her to do whatever made her happy.

"Wyatt, what are you doing?"

They bypassed the bed and entered a foyer that led to a massive master bathroom. She was sure she could put her whole apartment in this room. There were two of everything, which was the way Wyatt seemed to roll, having twins and all: two long granite counters with dual sinks, two toilets and two walk-in closets. Just one tub though, sunken and luxurious, surely big enough for two consenting adults to share. The thought made her hot all over.

He picked her up and set her on the countertop. "Gosh, you've got to stop doing that," she blurted.

"Doing what?" he asked, distracted. He was busy gathering supplies, peroxide, washcloths and a first aid kit.

"Carrying me places."

"You don't seem to have sense enough to keep yourself out of harm's way."

"I keep out of harm's way."

He snorted.

"I said I was sorry. I never meant to endanger your children. I wasn't…thinking."

"There's a lot of that going around."

Did he mean the night they'd slept together? Was he regretting it? Of course he was. She'd been nothing but trouble from the moment they'd met.

He placed a warm washcloth on her forehead, and she flinched.

"Sorry, Brooke. I've got to clean this wound."

"It's nothing."

"Nothing?" He placed his hands on her shoulders and swiveled her partway around. She got a good look at her wound in the light.

"Oh!" It was three times the size she'd seen in the car's mirror. Blood had caked on her forehead. It looked like a red rose atop a lumpy cupcake. Only this was not sweet. "I didn't realize."

"You could've been seriously hurt," he said through tight lips. He dabbed at the blood some more.

"But I wasn't. I never expected you to drag your babies out into the storm to rescue me."

"You left me no choice. What else was I supposed to do? Let you crash your car and get hurt or…or—"

"You put your children in danger for me."

"I could let you believe that. It would serve you right. But the truth is, I know the land and the four-wheel-drive Jeep has weathered lots of storms. I wouldn't deliberately put my kids in danger."

"But still, you dragged them out of bed to come get me."

"I won't be disagreeing with you."

"I'm so sorry, Wyatt. I promise you won't know I'm here and in the morning I'll—"

"You're not going anywhere in the morning, Brooke. This storm is pounding the land, and the weather reports aren't good. Looks like we're in for a few more days of it. There's another storm right behind this one."

"There is?" She took a swallow.

"I'm afraid so."

He finished washing her wound and dried her forehead, then took a pad of gauze and soaked it with peroxide. "This is gonna sting a bit," he said.

"You're going to love every second of it."

He leaned back to look into her eyes. His were still cold, hard and so amazingly blue, she wanted to cry. But she'd already done enough crying. She'd take her medicine like a big girl and pay the price for her stupidity.

"You should've listened to me. Then none of this would've happened. You put your life in danger, Brooke."

And then she got it. She knew why he'd come after her. She'd put him in a terrible position. Shoot. She wished she was wrong on this, but her heart told her the truth. He couldn't let her go it alone to possibly crash her car or worse. His wife had died in a car crash. Those memories must have tortured him tonight. Wyatt couldn't stand by and let another woman die on his watch. He had to come after her; his conscience wouldn't allow anything else. And whatever he'd said to the contrary, he *had* risked his kids and his own safety to rescue her.

"Ouch!"

The hardness in his eyes evaporated some. "I told you it would sting."

She almost choked on the pungent smell of peroxide. When he finished ministering to her gash, he capped the bottle and put it away. She jumped down from the counter before he picked her up again.

"It only lasts a minute or two," he said.

She nodded. "I'm really sorry I behaved so selfishly. Really, Wyatt. I wish there was a way for me to make it up to you."

His dark blond brows rose and the intense glint in his eyes put wicked thoughts in her head. Was he thinking about their night together? When they had labored long and hard to satisfy each other's hunger? When they'd spoken of nothing consequential and yet said so many things in the heat of passion?

Wyatt's landline phone rang in the master bedroom, breaking up the moment.

He walked over to it and glanced at the number, then

winced, his frown even deeper than the one he had for Brooke.

"I'll leave you so you can answer that."

"No, it's not necessary. I'll return that call in the morning. Right now, you're going to eat something."

"I'm not—" She was about to say she wasn't hungry, but then she remembered the life inside her needed nourishing. She'd been selfish enough tonight. She needed to eat, if only to maintain her strength for the baby. "Okay, yes. It's a shame to let the dinner go to waste."

"Fine," he said. "And you should put some ice on that bump."

"Right. Ice. Just what I need. Gotcha."

He turned around at her sarcasm, and that brow rose again. Did he have to be so darn appealing, even when he was scowling at her?

She made the gesture of zipping her lip with her fingers.

Wyatt's eyes gleamed and a smile threatened to emerge on his face, before he turned around and kept going.

She followed behind without another word.

Dinner was a quiet affair of stilted conversation and reheated food. Nevertheless, she downed her meal with gusto. It was either a result of Henrietta's expert cooking or the fact that Brooke was eating for two now. She filled her tummy with chicken piccata, scalloped potatoes, yeast rolls and salad until she thought she would explode. "My compliments to the cook," she said once she was all through.

"I'll tell Henrietta. It'll earn me brownie points, relaying the compliment," Wyatt said, sipping coffee. He hadn't looked at her during the dinner. The vibe she got was that she'd pissed him off and now he was stuck with her. What was his demeanor saying? Don't mess with Texas? Or Texans, for that matter.

She kept her lips buttoned and spoke only when spoken to.

"How do you know about white noise?" he asked finally, pushing away his empty coffee cup.

She shrugged. "Years of babysitting, I guess. You pick up hints and tricks along the way. And I've been doing some reading. My, uh, sister-in-law Emma is pregnant."

And so am I. If only she had the courage to make that announcement.

"I'd never heard of it," he said, staring at her mystified. "There's so much…"

"You learn as you go, Wyatt."

"I suppose. But sometimes I feel behind the eight ball on all this."

"You're a businessman with a company to run. You can't possibly keep up on the latest baby trends. And the old ways of doing things aren't so bad."

He pushed his hands through his hair. "You mean like rocking a baby to sleep instead of brainwashing them with digital noise?"

She laughed. "Yes. Both ways work."

He chuckled, too, and his whole demeanor changed. It was nice to see his smile again, if only for a few seconds. She could faint dead away from how his eyes touched upon hers. They lingered for a while, sparkling brilliant blue like the sea on a sunny day. It was killer to see him unguarded and free of any pain or anger.

"So are you hating me right now, or have I moved up the scale to mild dislike?" she finally asked.

A deep sigh broke from his throat. "Brooke."

"I'm sorry. But we are going to be stuck here together for a few days."

He shook his head at her comment. "I don't hate anyone. Dislike is reserved for my enemies."

"You have enemies?" Now that was a surprise.

"A few. You can't get to this level in business without ruffling feathers and pissing people off. I've done my share of negotiating but I've always done it fairly. Some of my competitors haven't been so scrupulous. I don't abide ruthlessness in business or anywhere else."

"So, you dislike your competitors. That's probably the case for a lot of business owners. What did they do, undermine your good name?"

"I can fend for myself. And my name is just fine. But they hit me the hardest when Madelyn died. I was struggling with her loss and my babies being motherless, and my rivals swooped in during a vulnerable time in my life to steal contracts away. At the time, I was too grief-stricken to take much notice or to care."

"That sucks, Wyatt. That's a really rotten thing to do. Okay, so I'm not in that category. Thank God."

"Brooke, there's no need to put a name on any of this. I sure as hell don't know what to call...us." He gestured with his hands to both of them.

Us? As in, the two of them? Brooke wouldn't get her hopes up that he meant anything serious by using the term. There was just no other way to describe the two of them. Still, while they were on the subject of babies and white noise and all, why couldn't she bring herself to tell him she was carrying his child?

And the devil's voice in her head was only too glad to explain, *Because you couldn't bear for your baby to be unwanted, the way you were.* And that was the crux of the matter. She was just coming to terms with being pregnant herself, and having Wyatt rebuff and reject the baby would be a knife to her heart.

Outside, the storm didn't let up. Windows rattled and winds howled with frenetic energy. It was the gloomiest of gloomy and yet there they were having a cozy meal together in the warmth of the house with two sweet babies asleep in their cribs upstairs.

"Do you have to check on the animals or anything?"

Wyatt ground his teeth and nodded as if she'd hit upon the very thing he'd been thinking. "I probably should, but I..."

But he didn't want to leave the babies alone with a stranger. She would remedy that right now. If there was one thing she could do for him, it was that. "I'll watch the twins, Wyatt. I'll sit in their room if you'd like. And I promise no more stunts. I'll be right there if they need something. Although I wasn't hinting for you to go out in this god-awful weather."

"The weather doesn't bother me, but I should check on the horses in the barn at the very least. I've gotta make sure they have feed and water. And it's not necessary for you to sit with the babies. I'll look in on them before I go out. They should sleep the rest of the night. Why don't you get ready for bed? You must be tired. You can listen for them in the guest bedroom."

She was exhausted. And the idea of cuddling up with a pillow and a warm blanket over her suddenly became appealing. Usually a night owl, her energy cells shut down after nine o'clock these days.

"Sounds good. But first, let me help put some of these things away," she said.

Wyatt didn't stop her from picking up plates and taking them to the kitchen. They worked silently, moving about the room tidying up and making very sure they didn't accidentally bump into each other. She couldn't have him touching her tonight, not while the storm raged outside and her innermost feelings were so close to the surface. She liked Wyatt a whole lot, and the iron barriers she usually put up with men seemed to falter when he was near. And that was a bad, bad thing.

"Follow me. I'll get you something to wear for the night."

He was halfway up the stairs before she started the climb, trying to keep her eyes down and not on the precise cut of his jeans and the rear end that was pretty near perfection. It was darn hard not to notice as his boots clicked and clacked upon the shiny wood steps, accentuating what was going on with every long-legged stride he took. Then she caught a glimpse of his shoulders in the tight cotton shirt. He was one of those cowboys whose muscles bunched under the shirtsleeves.

It wasn't as if she hadn't seen him naked. But somehow this was more intimate: being alone with him in his home with his children sleeping just steps away from her room.

"Here we are," he said, once he reached the room that was two doors down from the nursery and on the opposite side of the hallway from his master bedroom. "You can bed down in here. There's new toothbrushes and towels and everything you might need. If you don't find something, just let me know."

"I'm sure it's fine. Thanks."

"Oh," he said, remembering something. "Just a sec."

He walked away and then came back holding a red plaid flannel shirt. "This is the best I can do right now. It's clean."

She'd wondered if he would give her one of his wife's garments to wear, or if he still had any of her clothes around. Wearing something that was Madelyn's would be too darn weird, so the flannel shirt was a good choice.

He handed it to her and she hugged it to her chest. "Thanks."

Maybe hugging his shirt wasn't the brightest idea. His gaze dipped down to her chest and his eyes flickered like a newly lit flame.

She took a big breath.

He did the same. "Well," he said, lifting his eyes to meet hers.

"Well," she said, captivated.

He made a face, then pushed his hand through his hair. "I'd best go see to the animals."

"And the twins?"

"Are sleeping tight. But you can check on them if you'd like while I'm gone. I hope to be only ten minutes or so."

"Fine, I'll be listening for them."

"Appreciate that."

Five

It was a mother of a storm. Wyatt wasn't a small man, and yet as he exited the warmth of his home, he was thrashed about quite handily by sweeping thirty-mile-an-hour gusts that nearly stole his hat from his head. He pushed it down with the flat of his hand and trudged toward the barns. He had a string of Arabians that wouldn't take kindly to Mother Nature's outburst. A few years back, he'd installed floor heating in the barn, but those animals were feisty and high-strung and they sure as hell didn't like the boom of thunder and the sound of rain pelting the rooftops overhead. It was not quite hurricane weather, and he was grateful he had the means and the cash to provide the best structures for the animals. If the cattle had any sense, they'd take shelter in the overhangs on the property he'd set up every forty acres or so to provide a source of cover for his crew.

He reached the barn and made quick work of checking on the horses, pitchforking a layer of extra straw in their stalls, and making sure they had enough alfalfa and oats to fill their bellies. It would be at least two days before his crew would return. His weekend crew couldn't get onto the ranch anyway, and he'd texted them all earlier, telling them not to try. It was too dangerous.

With his work done, he latched the barn doors. He fought his way back, putting his head down and trudging through winds that could likely lift him off the ground and carry him to parts unknown. But he made it to the house just fine.

He stood in the foyer, shedding his cold, rain-soaked coat and gloves. The warmth inside the house seeped into his bones. It would take a hot shower to completely thaw him out.

He climbed the stairs two at a time, ready for this night to be over, and checked on the babies. But he damn well wasn't prepared for the sight before his eyes. He halted and swallowed hard.

Brooke.

She was leaning over Brianna's crib, her mile-long tanned legs giving him quite a show. As she bent further, he caught a powerful glimpse of the slip of white cotton panties she wore and the plump, perfect cheeks peeking out.

He blew breath out of his lungs and admired the view, his groin tightening up, his heart racing. What he wouldn't give to have her here under different circumstances. To have the freedom to take her to his bed and make wild love to her again and again.

He groaned, the sound penetrating the room, to his chagrin.

Brooke startled and turned around, catching him in the act of lusting after her. She gasped, a beautiful breathy sound that stirred his senses even more as they met eye to eye across the darkened room.

Brianna quieted back to sleep, thanks to Brooke, and then Wyatt remembered his place, the fact that Brooke wasn't here by choice and that he wasn't available to her. Not in the way he craved. But judging by the spark of heat in Brooke's eyes she tried to conceal, she might be craving him, too.

She tiptoed out of the room, edging her way past him in the doorway, her breasts teasing his chest as she passed by. That wisp of a touch nearly undid him.

"Brooke."

She whirled around, her eyes knowing and hungry. "She was fussing. I calmed her back to sleep."

"Thanks."

"You're cold and wet," she said. He liked having her eyes on him.

"I'm getting ready for a warm shower."

She nibbled on her very plump bottom lip and drew his attention there. "Good idea."

Crap. Did she have to have such a kissable mouth? Now all he could think about was kissing her senseless, stripping her of his shirt and having her join him in the shower.

"I'll be off to bed now," she said, without making a move.

"I, uh…okay."

The staring match continued. Wyatt could look into her pretty coffee-brown eyes all night. Her hair was falling off one shoulder, all those lush rich raven strands close enough to reach out and touch.

"Brooke," he said again, giving his head a regretful shake.

"I know, Wyatt. It's okay… Good night."

He sucked in air. She felt it, too, and there wasn't a damn thing either of them could do about it. "Night."

Finally, she turned and headed down the hallway to

her own room. Before closing the door, she wiggled her fingers at him.

Once she was out of sight, Wyatt breathed a sigh of relief. Two more days of this could mean trouble. What a freaking mess he was. Hungering for another woman in the very home he'd once shared with Madelyn.

It wasn't going to happen.

But oh, it wasn't going to be easy, either.

When morning dawned, the sky was just as dreary as the night before. There was no sign of sunshine, just gray threatening clouds. A steady light cascade thudded against the roof, but without the theatrics of thunder and lightning. Today's storm was the second-class citizen to yesterday's deluge.

Wyatt pulled himself out of bed, splashed water on his face and shoulders, toweled off, threw on a pair of jeans and a shirt, and padded barefoot to the nursery. Would Brooke be in there again wearing his shirt and nothing else? A small tortured part of him sorta hoped so, crazy glutton for punishment that he was. But as he stepped into the room, he saw that only his precious two were in there, still sleeping. Brianna was on her back, looking so much like her mother it pained him. Her hair was the same honey blond with slight curls and her eyes were shaped like almonds, wide across her little face. She had the same fair complexion and sweet smile as her mother, and it melted his heart every time he looked at her. Brett was blond, too, but his hair was a darker shade that might just change to light brown when he got older. He was a good mix of both Wyatt and Madelyn, although people who didn't know Madelyn thought his son looked exactly like him, which made him puff up with pride.

He smiled and exited the room. Any minute now, they'd wake and all hell would break loose. It was always the same, the welcome quiet before the toddler storm. And he'd learned to take advantage of these quiet times. Having a cup of coffee in peace was a luxury. He descended the staircase, smacking his lips over the prospect of a simple bowl of cereal and a steamy brew. As he neared the kitchen, the scent of coffee filled his nostrils.

Before he could gather his thoughts, a sassy female voice greeted him. "Morning, sleepyhead."

He entered the kitchen, smiling. But his fantasies were extinguished quickly. Brooke was wearing the same clothes she'd been in last night, only this time, her silvery silk blouse wasn't tucked in. "Sleepyhead? It's six in the morning."

"I thought cowboys rose at the crack of dawn."

He glanced out the window. "Today, who could tell?"

She chuckled. "You got me there. It's nasty out there. Want some coffee? Oh, I hope you don't mind, but I sort of helped myself to your kitchen. I've got bacon under the broiler and I was going to crack some eggs. Are you in?"

"I don't mind at all. I figured cereal would be my breakfast and lunch of choice without Henrietta. Hell yeah to coffee, and I'm *all* in. How's the head?"

"Surprisingly, not bad. I thought I'd wake up to a huge headache. I guess I got lucky."

"You got damn lucky." Her hair covered her bruise. He imagined it had turned fifty shades of purple by now.

"How long do you suppose we have?" she asked.

Wyatt knew exactly what she meant. "Maybe fifteen minutes, maybe half an hour. The kids usually wake up around six thirty."

"Do they eat anything special?" she asked, pouring the coffee into the one mug she'd laid out on the counter.

"Well, they've been eating just about everything these days. So eggs and a bit of bacon is fine. I think Henrietta used to make them baby oatmeal or something. "

"Okay, we'll figure it out."

He liked the way Brooke took over his kitchen. She wasn't a wilting flower who needed to have everything handed to her. She'd stepped in and helped out and didn't seem uncomfortable in her surroundings.

"How did you sleep?" he asked, being a good host, though his mind automatically flashed back to an image of her lying next to him in that hotel bed. Things were different now and he knew it for fact, but his groin was having issues that didn't surprise him. He switched gears, thinking about his children sleeping innocently in their nursery right now. They were his splash of ice-cold water. They were the buffer he needed.

"Like a baby," she said. "The bed is comfy and the sound of the rain sorta lulled me to sleep. How about you?"

"Good. I slept good."

He removed the bacon from the broiler while she cooked the eggs. He made toast, too, and within a few minutes, they were sitting in the kitchen eating breakfast. "You're not having coffee?"

She shook her head, her gaze dipping to his chest. He hadn't buttoned up, and now he caught her stealing a glimpse. When his lips curved up in a smile, she pulled her gaze off him immediately and made a production of buttering her toast. "No, I, uh… I'm not one for coffee. I'm fine with orange juice. Want some?"

Her dark hair was in wild disarray, looking natural and untamed and gorgeous falling past her shoulders. He hadn't thought to give her a hairbrush last night. He had other things on his mind, such as how in hell he was going to steer clear of her this weekend.

"No thanks. I'm good." He sipped his coffee and they both concentrated on the meal, keeping the conversation to a minimum.

Cries erupted upstairs ten minutes later. "Peace as you

know it has just ended." He rose from his seat. "I'll go get them."

"I'll go with you."

Wyatt wasn't going to argue. When it came to his kids, without Henrietta here to guide him, he was on a bucking wild horse without a saddle.

Brooke scooped Brett up just before he slung his taxi-cab-yellow dump truck at Brianna's head. She took the truck out of his hands and twirled him around and around. "Here we go," she said, giving Brett an airplane ride. "Zoom, zoom." Brett's legs shot out and his giggles made Brianna stop attacking the seventy-inch flat screen's remote controller with a spoon to look up at her brother in envy.

"Your turn next," Brooke said, almost out of breath. The little ones weighed a good twenty-five pounds if they weighed one pound. Brooke figured this was the best work-out she'd get while she was here. Wyatt had offered her his private gym in the basement of the house, and maybe when the twins napped, she'd head down there to check it out, but until she got the okay from a doctor to do some mild exercise, all she would be doing was looking.

Brianna raced around the great room, which seemed to have inadvertently become the twins' playroom. As a matter of fact, every room downstairs had signs of tod-dler-dom. There were dolls and trucks, cars and dress-up clothes everywhere, though neatly arranged, thanks to Henrietta, Brooke presumed. Yet the entire stunning ranch home, with all the latest perks and privileges and modern digital conveniences, showed signs of children.

Not a bad thing at all. Maybe that's why Brooke felt comfortable instead of out of place here. The house was grand not but austere. So what if she didn't want to be here. She was stuck and she might as well make the best of it.

Brianna came running into her arms and she lifted her up and flew her across the room. "Zoom, zoom, zoom. You're flying, Bri." Sweet laughter poured from the child's tiny mouth and her joyous smile put a sparkle in her blue-bonnet eyes.

"Daddy, lookee me."

"I see, Bri. You're flying," Wyatt said. His eyes were filled with so much love, Brooke's heart lurched. This family was missing one vital part and she saw the hint of that sadness, even as Wyatt smiled at his daughter and held his son.

"I flied too," Brett said.

"Yes, you did," Brooke said, setting Brianna down and drawing deep breaths into her lungs.

Wyatt made note of her labored breathing and announced, "Okay, flying school is closed for today."

The children protested with whines and whimpers.

"But maybe if Daddy says it's okay, we can have ice cream?" She gave Wyatt a sheepish smile. "Is that okay?

"Yay, Daddy, pleeeeze," from Brianna.

"Pleeeeze, pleeeeze," Brett parroted.

"Oh, um…" He glanced at his watch. The children had eaten a good breakfast and lunch, and it was now approaching dinnertime. "Sure, why not?"

The twins squealed with joy. Wyatt lifted Brett in one arm, and picked up Brianna in the other, giving Brooke a break as they headed for the kitchen.

Twenty minutes later, the ceiling had nearly caved in from Brianna's screams and Brett was covered from head to toe in fudgy ice cream. There wasn't a clean spot on his shirt, despite the bib. Apparently bibs weren't fool-proof, not with little hands pulling and tugging at them constantly.

"Okay, well, maybe ice cream wasn't such a bright idea," Brooke said.

"You think?" Wyatt frowned at the mess that was his kitchen, splattered walls and all.

"I'll take care of it. You mentioned you have work to do?"

"I can't leave you with this...them." He spread his arms out wide. Which only made her want to jump into them. Getting away from him today would be imperative for her peace of mind. They'd been together all day, dealing with the children, and she'd been all too aware of him. His presence beside her. His heart-stealing blue eyes. The intoxicating scent of his cologne. When he was close she felt safe, and that scared her most of all. She couldn't give up her heart again. She was scarred by Royce's deception and didn't trust herself to make the right decisions when it came to men. Especially since she had no idea what Wyatt would say about the baby she carried. And she was too chicken to find out.

At times, she'd catch him ogling her with an intense look that even she, a novice when it came to knowing a man's mind, understood as hunger and desire. And her ego would rocket like a shooting star.

Wyatt looked ready to escape the chaos. He was struggling to balance his fatherly duties with tending to business.

"Wyatt, I can manage just fine. Piece of cake."

"Oh, yeah? What's your plan?"

"My plan? Well, a bubble bath works wonders."

His brows arched and he gave her a sardonic smile. "Sounds perfect."

"For them, Wyatt."

"Oh, right." At least he could tease about the tension that sizzled between them, despite the double kid duty. "I knew that."

Her ego soared again.

"I don't know." He scrubbed his face, pulling at the

golden stubble on his jaw. "It's a lot to ask of you. They're a handful and a half."

"Hey, it's not as if you're far away. Your office is down here, isn't it?" she asked over Brianna's meltdown.

"Yep, but it's in another wing of the house."

"You have an intercom system, right? I'll use it if I need to. And that's a promise. Now go, and let me put these little ones out of their misery."

And you out of yours.

He finally agreed. After he helped get the twins upstairs, she took over, giving them both a bath full of light airy bubbles. The kids immediately simmered down, their sugar high from the ice cream leveling off. Brooke splashed them silly, until the room filled with their giggles, until their little fingers and toes shriveled to wrinkled raisins. When the bath was over, Brooke wrapped each one in a My Little Pony towel and snuggled them to her chest, drying them off. She dressed them in their jammies and then all three squatted on the floor to play. The twins had so many toys, and they played with each and every one before they got bored of the games. Then Brooke laid them down on a pastel-colored quilt and sang them silly songs. When she couldn't remember the lyrics, she made up the words, and every song brought big grins to their faces.

"Piece of cake?"

She swiveled her head to find Wyatt blocking the doorway, his arms folded across his chest, blue eyes filled with admiration.

"Putty in my hands," she said.

"I know the feeling," he said under his breath.

Oh, God.

"Actually, I know the *secret*," she said.

"And what's that?"

He came to sit beside her and ruffled both of the children's hair. Again, those blue eyes were alight with love for his kids.

"Play with them 24/7. Entertain and delight them, give them what they want."

"And exhaust yourself…"

"Do I look exhausted?" She turned her face to him. When their eyes met, his nearness suddenly made it very hot in the room. It was a mistake to ask him that leading question, because his expression went dewy soft and he reached out to touch a strand of her hair. Focusing on the dark lock, he shook his head. "No," he rasped. "You look beautiful."

He touched her then, with his smile.

She gave him an uncertain smile back. "Thank you."

He backed off, noting her hesitation. "You've been up here two hours."

"Really? I lost track of time. Probably should think about dinner."

He nodded and cleared his throat before standing up. He reached for her hand and helped her rise. Pretending nonchalance, she pulled her hand away and made a fuss about cleaning up the room when all she wanted was for him to touch her and keep on touching her.

Dangerous thoughts.

"Come on, you two. Let's race and see who can put the toys away the fastest." She dumped the first one into the toy box and the twins followed suit, grabbing toys two at a time, competing in another fun game.

Forty-five minutes later, Brooke and Wyatt were eating spaghetti in the kitchen with the twins. "Good move, not giving them sauce," Wyatt said.

"Butter and cheese keep the bath monster away."

He chuckled. "Yeah, you sure are an arsenal of helpful hints."

"Maybe when dealing with children." The same couldn't

be said in her dealings with men. In that regard, she was clueless.

Wyatt tipped his head to stare at her, a question in his eyes.

"That didn't come out right," she said, easing diced pasta into Brett's mouth as Wyatt fed Bri. It was a subject that needed changing quickly. "Hey, looks like these guys are ready to conk out. I bet they go to sleep right after dinner. Then you can finish up your work."

"I'm finished for the day," he said.

Oh, great. It was coming up on eight o'clock. Too early to turn in. Of course, Brooke could claim fatigue and watch television in her room or read a book.

"I thought I'd get a fire going, relax some and have hot chocolate," he said, giving her a glance.

"With marshmallows? Gosh, that sounds like heaven," she cooed, thinking out loud. Peace and quiet by a crackling fire, sipping hot chocolate, and relaxing with Wyatt after a long, tiresome day would be pretty amazing. Hot chocolate was something she *could* drink and not endanger her baby. But uh-oh, she'd just stepped in it. Now there was no legitimate way out without sounding lame.

"With marshmallows," he said on a nod. "Then you'll join me?"

When would she ever learn to button her lips?

"Uh, yeah. For a little while. Unless you'd rather be alone, with your, uh, thoughts?"

He grinned. "Men never want to be alone with their thoughts."

"Okay, then."

As expected, the twins had fallen asleep right after dinner without much coaxing. Now the big ranch house was quiet. She padded on bare feet down the stairs, wearing Wyatt's ginormous flannel plaid robe, which tied around her waist twice. The robe hugged her like a big teddy bear, a teddy bear that sported Wyatt's appealing scent. She'd been wearing the same outfit for two days straight and had asked Wyatt for something to throw on over his shirt while she laundered her clothes. The rain hadn't let up; just as the weatherman had predicted, a new storm had piggybacked on this one.

She entered the living room, where a floor-to-ceiling bedrock fireplace blazed. "It's beautiful in here," she said, hugging herself around the middle. The entire room was softly lit by the glow of the fire. Wyatt looked up from his place on the floor and gave her a heart-melting smile. Two mugs of steamy hot chocolate sat on the hearth, a bag of marshmallows beside them. "Have a seat," he said, and arched a brow when she sat down on the floor, leaning her body against the part of the sofa farthest away from him. He couldn't think she'd sit directly next to him, could he? Not in this lifetime. It was hard enough seeing him all day, as he interacted with his children and sauntered about in those perfect-fitting jeans, with that sexy pirate beard going on. A girl could only take so much.

"At least move closer to the fire," he said, a knowing tone in his voice. "It'll warm you."

"I'm warm enough, thank you very much."

"Suit yourself."

He sprinkled mini marshmallows into both mugs and handed her one. Then he leaned back against the sofa and stretched out his long legs. Sipping the cocoa, he quietly watched the fire for a while. "Don't get much peace around here. This is nice."

"It is."

"You're good with the little ones," he said.

"They're precious, Wyatt."

"They're all I have left…"

She let that comment go, but she knew he was thinking of their mother, Madelyn. Oh, to be loved like that, so strongly that even in death the bond couldn't be broken.

He put his head down. "Sorry."

"No need to be, Wyatt. You went through a trauma. All of you did, and I get it."

"It's just that… I'm feeling all this guilt now." His eyes lost their gleam, and he looked absolutely miserable.

"Guilt? About what happened between us?" Her stomach clenched. At times, she forgot she was carrying his child, but the baby made his presence known. Her breasts were becoming increasingly tender. She got tired more easily now, and she often bordered on nausea, especially in the morning. As far as symptoms went, hers were mild, but they were there reminding her daily that she couldn't just pretend all was right with the world. Not until she shed her secret. She wanted to tell him to forget about what had happened between them, to put it in the past and save himself from his torment, but she couldn't. She couldn't say those words when she had more profound words to say.

"About what I'm feeling now. About how much I want you, Brooke."

Her hand shook and the mug nearly tipped on its way to her mouth. Goodness, he'd just come right out and spoken his mind. She wished it would be that easy for her. She set her mug down and stared at the marshmallow circles melting as fast as her heart. "What if I said…the feeling is mutual, but we both know better?"

"Do we?" he asked, his voice registering doubt. She glanced at him again, and his dubious expression caught her off guard. Firelight reflected in his eyes and she noted the torment in them. His expression gave her pause.

"What do I say to that, Wyatt?"

"I don't know. Maybe one of us needs to be reckless," he added.

"I thought both of us were, at the wedding."

His Adam's apple bobbed up and down as he swallowed. "Meeting you that night was the best thing that happened to me in nine months. You helped me through a rough time, and I'll be forever grateful."

She didn't want his gratitude. What exactly did she want from Wyatt? She knew the score. He was emotionally unavailable and she'd be fooling herself to think anything else. She was pregnant and a little bit frightened about telling him, because then they'd have to face reality and make appropriate arrangements for custody and all the ugly painstaking plans that went along with a child being born out of wedlock. Gosh, it was so much easier to put her head in the sand and not deal with any of this. Pretty soon, her body would betray her with a belly bump that would expand, and then she'd have no choice but to reveal her pregnancy. But tonight she wanted to sip hot chocolate with Wyatt and just *be*.

She heard one of the babies' cries from upstairs and just *being* was immediately eighty-sixed. "Is that Brianna crying?" she asked softly, her ears perking up.

"I think it's Brett," Wyatt said, putting his mug down and listening. "Yep, that's him. Bri will be right behind him. She doesn't sleep when he's in a state. Stay here by the fire. I'll see to them." Wyatt popped up.

"I'll help." She rose and nodded. "It's okay. I want to."

"Appreciate that. Double rocking them doesn't always work."

"I can't see how it ever works, Wyatt. What do you do, hold one in each arm?"

"I try." He sighed. "Usually Henrietta is here to help out."

He really did need a nanny. Or two. How could one aging housekeeper keep pace with twins? Brooke was younger by thirty years, and even she was exhausted after watching them most of the day.

As she followed him up the staircase, Brianna started wailing. Now both babies were rocking the nursery walls. Wyatt and Brooke entered the room and she took one quick, assessing look at Brett. "He's soaked through his jammies."

"Ah," Wyatt said. "That explains it."

"I'll change him and get him back to sleep," she said. "Why don't you rock Brianna?"

"Sounds good. If you're sure…"

"I'm sure."

And then on an afterthought, a storm of indecision crossed his face. "Their mother didn't want the babies separated. In a house this size, they could each have their own room, but Madelyn thought this way was best."

"There's time for them to have their own rooms later in life. I think it's a good plan for now, Wyatt. Twins have a special bond, I think."

He let out a relieved sigh. "Okay."

The poor guy. He was second-guessing his decisions regarding his kids and trying like mad to honor his late wife's wishes.

"You take the rocker, Brooke. I'll walk Brianna in my arms. She likes that."

Twenty minutes later, Brett was dressed in clean pajamas and sleeping soundly. Wyatt wasn't far behind putting his daughter back into her crib and covering her. He kissed her forehead so lightly, it might have been an air kiss, and then did the same to Brett.

With a hand to Brooke's back, he guided her out of the room and down the hall. "Thanks," he said. She found herself wrapped in his cushy robe, standing just outside her bedroom door. "You've been pretty darn great. I'd kiss you good-night, but we both know where that would lead."

Her lips formed into a pout. She couldn't hide her disappointment. She felt closer to Wyatt tonight. Maybe it was the intimacy of putting his little ones to sleep and working as a team, sharing meals and personal thoughts. Maybe it was the strong pull of his deep gaze that told her beyond words how much he wished things were different.

Maybe it was his body language and the way his eyes were on her mouth now, looking as if he'd devour her if given the chance.

"What if *I* kissed *you*, Wyatt?" She rose up on tiptoes, absorbing the heat of his skin as she laid her palm on his jaw. Not giving him a chance to answer, she brushed her lips over his.

"Good night," she whispered, and as she backed away, Wyatt's lids lowered, his breath rushed out in a groan, and before she knew what was happening, he reached out and pulled her into his arms. As he crushed her against his chest, his mouth came down on hers and his kiss stole her very breath. It wasn't hard to melt into him, to give up her denials and simply feel. And oh, how good it was.

"God, Brooke," he rasped over her lips, and then drove into her mouth in a fiery surge that she met with equal eagerness and enthusiasm.

"Wyatt," she murmured, raking her fingers through the short tufts of his hair.

The connection between them might only be physical but it was strong, real and overpowering, judging by how fast her heart was racing, how every nerve in her body was standing on end.

He cupped her face with both hands and positioned her head to give him more access.

His kisses went deep, and raw, elemental lust rose up. Suddenly, she wanted his hands all over her again; she wanted to feel his flesh against hers and have him inside her making her splinter apart.

He gripped the tie of her robe to pull her closer. "I've been wondering all night what you have on under here."

"Not too much," she offered softly, the need in her voice ringing in her ears.

A painful groan emerged from his throat. "That's what I thought."

He kissed her again, his mouth ravaging and greedy. She didn't mind being the recipient of his hot, passionate hunger. She wasn't going to stop him. She wasn't going to let any rational thoughts enter her head. Not tonight.

"I don't think I can walk away from you tonight, Brooke."

Her chin up, she captured his gaze. "I don't think I'd let you."

She turned the knob on her bedroom door and entered backward, keeping his face in her line of vision the entire time. He followed her, and the door flew shut with a kick of his foot.

He came toward her, stalking her like a wild animal, limber in his approach. His blue gaze was as dark as midnight. He tugged her forward by the sash on her robe. It opened and hung from her shoulders, the cool evening air replacing the warm furnace of material and leaving her naked but for the panties she wore.

Wyatt sucked in a breath and gave her a glowing look of admiration. Then he sifted through the material of the robe and laid his hand on her breast. She closed her eyes from the pleasure of his touch. And when he began a slow, deliberate massage with the flat of his palm, squeezing the skin together and flicking her nipple, everything below her waist began to throb. Like crazy. Sweat broke out on her forehead.

"Are you sure about this?" he asked.

Totally not fair of him to ask. "Yes. Oh, yes."

Six

Wyatt's hands roamed her body as his kisses drove her to the brink. It wasn't any different, any less urgent, than the night they'd shared at the inn. In the guest room of his beautiful ranch home, amid horses and cattle and yes, children sleeping a few rooms away, she gave in to the storm of desire enveloping her with a force that she could no longer fight. If she was being stupid and foolish, then so be it. She'd pay the price later, but for now, in this moment, she wanted Wyatt. No, she *needed* Wyatt.

A shudder passed through her entire body. Wanting was one thing, but needing him? Fear slammed into her heart and brought her up short momentarily. The blood froze in her veins.

Wyatt immediately stopped midkiss. He sensed something was up, and didn't that tell her all she needed to know about him? He was sensitive enough to know she'd balked. "What's wrong, darlin'?"

The corners of her mouth lifted as she touched his

cheek, her palm grazing the rough stubble of his beard. His eyes bore down on her, waiting. "Nothing."

He pulled her palm to his mouth and kissed the inside of her hand. "You sure?"

She nodded, plastering on a smile. "Positive."

Other than she was falling hard for the Texan, the father of twins and her unborn baby, and there was nothing she could do to stop it.

He gave her a soft, loving kiss and murmured. "Climb into bed, sweetheart. Stay warm. I'll be right back."

She was pretty sure he was going to his room to get protection. Oh, man.

After he left, she gazed out the window at threatening stark gray clouds and the pouring rain that was keeping her trapped here. Now, that was a notion: being shut in with a gorgeous guy who you're pretty sure is the best man you'd ever met in your life. Only he was still hung up on his late wife. And he'd made it clear in no uncertain terms, quite a few times, that having two children was quite enough for him.

The debate in her head raged like the storm outside. She pulled the material of her robe together tightly, and crossed her arms over her chest, ready to tell Wyatt everything and pay the consequences.

And then, there he was standing in the doorway, shirtless, bootless, in jeans riding low on his waist, holding a batch of purple-hued flowers in his hand. His hair was damp and there were raindrops sprinkled on his bare shoulders.

"These are for you, Brooke," he said. His eyes blazed bright blue as he sauntered over to her and set the flowers in her hand.

"They're beautiful," she said. "Where did you get them?"

"Out back. There's a garden, and these are pretty hardy

this time of year. Asters and violets. This one here is a tiger lily."

She stared at the flowers as he pointed them out.

"I figured you might like them."

She pressed them to her chest and felt tears coming on. "I love them, Wyatt. You went out in the rain for these?"

"You deserve them," he said. "I, uh, wanted you to know, I'm not the jerk who ran out on you at the inn."

"I think I know that now."

As her arms slid down her sides, the robe opened again. Now both of them were standing in the middle of the room, nearly naked. He began rubbing her arms up and down briskly, getting her circulation going and heating her up inside. "I thought you'd be in bed. Aren't you freezing?"

"I, uh, no. You're pretty good at keeping me warm."

"Ah, Brooke," he said, circling his arms around her entire body, warming her with his own heat. "I like the sound of that."

And then his kisses rained down on her and for all those beautiful minutes, she kissed him back, loving the taste of him, loving the poignant sound of his passion-filled groans, loving the way he held her as though she was precious and sacred.

They moved to the bed together, locked in each other's arms. Wyatt gently removed the robe from her shoulders and lowered her down until the mattress met with her bare back and the pillow cradled her head. He loomed above her, all those straining muscles holding him back from crushing her with his body, and brought his mouth down to hers. He smelled of fresh rain and outdoors, and she roped her arms around his neck and played with the dark blond strands of his hair.

He began to lightly massage her shoulders. His fingertips dug in to release tension there before he moved lower still to caress her tender breasts. Smoothing them over with gentle hands brought relief, and then he molded them with a propping motion making ready to take her into his mouth. She held her breath, waiting. And then he dipped his head and sucked on her, his tongue circling the round orb and lashing her with moisture. An almost painful pleasure coursed down to her belly, and a tiny moan escaped her lips.

Down below, his erection strained against his jeans and ground into her body, pulsing and ready. She thrashed her head against the pillow, biting her lip as electric currents outraced her heartbeats. "Wyatt," she breathed.

He tore his mouth away from her now-aching breast and slid down her body, pulling her free of her panties. Lifting her legs up, he positioned himself, and the hot, wet slide of his tongue teased her core. She stilled, absorbing the sensations washing through her like waves on the ocean, one right after another, his stroking creating tingles and light shocks.

"Oh," she whimpered, biting her lip.

Everything inside her tightened up and as his relentless tongue bathed her, her body absorbed the pleasure until it was too, too much. The pulses grew heavier, tighter, and then, then a spasm burst inside her and claimed her breath.

She hurtled back down to earth, sated, her body limp and her endorphins causing the highest high.

Wyatt released her then, his eyes glazed and hungry.

"So good," she said, instead of admitting it was the best.

He brought himself up, kissed her soundly on the lips and then rolled away to unzip his jeans. "I'm glad. It was for me, too."

He moved his pants down his legs and a sigh escaped her throat as she caught a glimpse of him in all his glory.

She rolled on her side and took him in her hand. "Thank you for the flowers," she whispered, and began long, slow, deliberate strokes. He was hot silk in her hands, so smooth, so inspiring. Scooting closer, she pressed her mouth to his and began kissing him. "Lie back and enjoy."

And if the grunts and noisy sounds he made were any indication, she was giving Wyatt just as much pleasure as he'd given her tonight.

"I'll never make it," he rasped, "if you go on doing what you're doing."

He gave her no time to respond. He flipped her over onto her back then, and she was captured by the inferno in Wyatt's eyes. With his knee, he parted her legs and rose over her. A heady rush of adrenaline pulsed through her veins. She remembered the last time they were joined; this was going to be equally good, if not better. She saw the promise in Wyatt's eyes and believed it.

He touched the tip of his manhood to her. "Oh, man, Brooke," he murmured so quietly, it was more of a sigh. Her breath caught in her throat. She couldn't manage a reply; she couldn't utter a word. Sensations rippled through her as he pushed deeper, giving her time to adjust, time to accept him.

She pulled him down to her mouth and kissed him. It was beautiful and crazy good and from then on, Wyatt locked in on her body and she was done for. Completely and utterly in his zone. She gave everything she had to him and then some.

The furious passion in his eyes, his hands exploring every part of her and his magnificent erection kept her body on the brink. She was close to combusting in the very best way. He pumped and she bucked, he grated and she rubbed, he climbed and she followed.

A vivid curse pushed from his lips and the word vibrated in her ears. Everything below her waist tightened.

Talk dirty to me, Wyatt. I can take it.

The fact that he'd lost a bit of control pushed her over

the edge. There was nothing higher, or better, than being at this same place with him. Going the distance together.

He lifted her hips from the bed, squeezing her cheeks tight with his powerful hands as he thrust deeper still.

"Oh…oh, Wyatt."

"We're here, Brooke."

Her spasms of release joined his, a continuing series of shudders and moans that filled her ears. They were in their own place now, a few moments of exquisite flurry shared equally. Her heart was racing like mad, her body tight.

Wyatt kissed her gently, his hands softly tangling in her hair as he whispered sweet words in her ear. When he lifted up and moved beside her on the bed, his heat evaporated and cool air touched her skin. But it didn't matter; she was flushed and hot enough to warm up Wyatt's entire ranch house.

Wyatt brushed hair from her cheeks. "You're beautiful, Brooke."

If he kept saying it, she might just believe it.

"And this was…"

He didn't finish. Brooke understood his dilemma, how he must be feeling. What happened between them was better than good, better than great. It was freaking amazing. But Wyatt's admitting that would be disrespectful to Madelyn in his eyes. That had to be it.

Right now, as she came down from the most satisfying blissful sex of her life, she didn't want to think too much. She hugged a pillow to her chest and faced him. "Wyatt, you don't have to say anything. I think we both know."

He stared up at the ceiling and when she thought he'd checked out, he slipped his hand over hers and held on until her eyes closed and she drifted off.

Wyatt was sex-starved and Brooke's appearance in his life was a scratch to his itch. Or so he thought. But as he lay beside her on the bed they'd shared last night, watching her chest rise and fall in deep slumber, the rosy hue he'd put on her face making her appear even more beautiful, he realized he was full of crap.

He wasn't going to get her out of his system anytime soon.

He wanted her here. But as Sunday morning dawned, the worst of the storm was gone, leaving only a light drizzle in its place that would slow to a stop sometime this afternoon. Texas sunshine would dry the land, and the bridge would be repaired and drivable again. By tomorrow, Brooke would be heading away from Blue Horizon Ranch and he would have to let her go.

As she rolled over, the sheet covering her fell away and her breasts teased his chest. The gentle scraping of her nipples stirred everything male inside him. *Shoot.* He was hard again and ready to take her once more.

Lazy eyes opened to him and she smiled. It was a sweet, aftermath-of-good-loving smile that tugged at his heart. She blew her messy brown locks out of her eyes on a soft puff of breath.

"Mornin'," he croaked.

She chuckled, stretching her arms over her head. "Yes, it is," she said on a long, sexy sigh. "You look good enough to eat, Wyatt."

His lips curved up in a smile. Brooke always surprised him. "I was thinking the same about you."

She rose on her elbows, and his gaze drifted to her small, round, perfect breasts. "Have you checked on the babies?" she asked.

"I have. Ten minutes ago. They're asleep."

"Is it still raining?" she asked, taking a peek out the window.

"Yep, drizzling."

"Guess you're stuck with me another day."

"Guess so." He leaned in, inches from her mouth, and whispered, "It's a hardship."

She tried to swat at him, but he was too fast and caught her wrist midmotion. "Now that I've snagged you, what will I do with you?"

"Whatever you want," she said coyly.

He snapped his eyes to her. "God, Brooke. You're killing me."

"Am I?" she asked, her smile gone, her dark brown eyes soft and steady on him.

"Yeah."

She looked under the sheet draped at his waist. "You seem very much alive from where I'm sitting."

"I am alive, when I'm with you." Rising over her, her pinned her arms above her head and held her there. Her lips parted slightly, and the intake of her breath told him she wanted him again. There would be no protest, and he wasn't gonna leave this bed without making love to her again.

One minute later, his cell phone buzzed. He had a mind to ignore it. But he gazed over at the lit-up screen on the nightstand and bit back a curse. It was his mother again. Man, she had bad timing. He'd dodged her call the other night and managed to leave her a voice mail afterward telling her everything was all right.

But Mom was nothing but persistent.

Brooke looked at the phone. "It's your mother. You should answer it, Wyatt. She's probably worried about the kids and the storm."

He backed away from Brooke and sat up on the bed, gritting his teeth. "Yeah, you're right. I'm sorry I have to get this."

"It's okay," Brooke assured him.

"Don't move a muscle. Not an inch. Okay?" he asked.

CHARLENE SANDS 109

Her arms were above her head, her breasts exposed and gorgeous. "I promise."

Releasing a low guttural groan from his throat, he picked up the phone, walked out of the room and ducked into another bedroom.

"Yeah, hi, Mom."

"Wyatt. I've been trying to reach you. Is everything all right? The storm is all over the news here in New York. Lord, I remember those hurricanes. I know how dangerous they can be. How are my grandbabies?"

"The babies are fine. We're staying in and the storm's ready to pass. Did you get my message?"

"Yes, but, honey, I needed to speak with you in person. You have to understand how I worry. I haven't seen Brett and Brianna in months. You know that I was planning on coming to Texas for the cancer foundation's big fund-raiser in Dallas, right?"

"Yes, I know, Mom."

"And I was going to come to the ranch for a visit after that?"

"Uh-huh." He began to feel an ache in the pit of his stomach. Something was up with her, and he wasn't going to like it.

"Well, my plans have changed. I'll be coming to Blue Horizon before the fund-raiser, rather than after. I should arrive day after tomorrow. I'll stay about a week."

His heart stopped. He'd thought he had at least a month before she arrived. "What?"

"Sorry for the short notice, but it's just worked out better this way."

"For who?" he asked.

"Now, Wyatt, you know I have a busy schedule. You're all alone there, except for my Henrietta, and well, I miss the babies so. Have you managed to find a nanny yet?"

"It's in the works, Mom. I'm getting close." It was a

lie. He had some interviews scheduled, but nothing was concrete yet.

"That's what you said the last time we spoke. And poor Henrietta is being run into the ground trying to keep pace with my precious grandkids. Honey, I know you don't think I'd do a good job, but my offer still stands. I'll come back to Texas to live. I'm willing to help out. There's nothing I'm doing here that can't be postponed or canceled if you really need me."

Wyatt always thought her offer was an idle threat, but lately, she'd been speaking more and more about moving back to Texas and leaving high society behind to care for her grandchildren. It was an offer that he'd patiently and tactfully refused on several occasions.

She'd hate it here. Genevieve Brandt wasn't meant for country living, and when Wyatt was growing up, she'd reminded him and his father daily of the sacrifice she'd made for love. She was a city girl, through and through. As soon as his father retired from Blue Horizon, she'd dragged him off the ranch and moved him to her hometown and the faster-paced city life of New York. George Taylor Brandt passed on three years ago, and Wyatt was convinced that if he'd stayed on the ranch he loved after his retirement, he would still be alive today.

"Mom, we're managing just fine." It was a blatant lie.

"We'll see, honey," she said, a dubious tone in her voice. "I can't wait to see you and the babies."

"Uh, same here, Mom."

After the call ended, Wyatt stared at the phone as dozens of thoughts filled his head. He had to do right by his kids. But having his mother move in with him wasn't the answer. Oh, yeah, he loved her. She'd been a good mother, and she did adore his children, but she was also high-maintenance and somewhat self-centered. And she would drive him absolutely nuts.

He shook his head and remembered Brooke, the stunner he had waiting for him in bed just steps away. She, too, drove him nuts, in another way entirely.

He left all that behind and returned to the bedroom.

"What's wrong?" Brooke asked the second he walked in. She read his expression and must've seen his concern.

He sat down on the bed and ran a hand through his hair, staring at the opposite wall. "You don't want to hear it."

"Sure I do." She covered up and took a place next to him on the bed.

"My mother is coming for a visit."

"That's a good thing, isn't it?"

"It is if it was only that. But I get the feeling she's coming to check up on me and the kids. And if she doesn't like what she sees, she might just stay on *to help out*."

He shuddered and Brooke bit back a laugh.

"It's not funny," he said, focusing on the Dalí print on the wall.

"I know." He appreciated that she managed not to chuckle again, though he must've looked pretty comical, sitting almost buck naked on the bed, twitching because his mother was coming for a visit.

"I've been trying to find just the right nanny to relieve Henrietta of her duties. A new housekeeper I can always find, but a nanny, someone to watch my kids all day, that person has to be special. And I haven't had any luck finding anyone that meets my requirements."

Someone who could stand in for Madelyn.

"Sorry, Wyatt. Those children are treasures and they do deserve someone special." Brooke laid her hand on his shoulder, and her warmth and comfort seeped into his skin. Her touch, or maybe just having her understand his situation, helped a great deal. With Brooke beside him, he didn't feel quite so alone and devastated.

He covered her hand and turned to give her a smile.

When she returned the smile, his body stirred and his mouth sought hers again. Kissing her helped untangle his mind, and he indulged over and over again. It seemed that he needed lots of untangling. And when kissing wasn't enough, he pushed her down onto the bed, pulled off the sheets and fell headlong into Brooke's willing arms.

Making love to Brooke McKay was the best medicine for what ailed him.

"I'll do it," Brooke announced, coming to stand over Wyatt on the bed. He looked edible, lying with his arms over his head, his eyes still dusted with sleep and his luscious muscled chest calling for her touch. Dawn was long since gone. She'd just finished checking on the twins. They rustled about and made sweet noises, on the verge of waking. Any second now, they'd be up and ready to start the day, and she and Wyatt wouldn't have a moment to gather their thoughts. That's when the idea came to her. She wasn't ready to leave Blue Horizon yet. She needed more time with Wyatt. "I'll stay on during your mother's visit and pretend to be the twins' nanny."

"What are you talking about, darlin'?"

"You need a nanny, Wyatt. I'm here. I've got nothing on my agenda until Dylan's movie wraps, and I owe you."

Wyatt sat up, hung his legs over the side of the bed and planted his hands on the edge of the mattress. "After last night, and this morning, I'm thinking I'm the one owing you."

He was teasing. They'd satisfied each other and there was no measure to that, no payment for deeds. "That was mutual and equal. Wasn't it?"

He gave her an earnest look. "Yeah. So what do think you owe me?"

"You came after me in the storm with your kids in the

car. I'll never forget that. You risked them to save me. It's the least I can do. I want to help."

He heaved a big sigh and ran his hands through his hair, tousling it even more. Bed head looked incredibly sexy on him. "How can I ask you to do that for me?"

"You're not asking. I'm offering."

He thought about it awhile as she stood there, her heart in her throat. God, he had to say yes. Once the offer was out there, she realized how very much she wanted him to agree. She wasn't ready to leave him. She wasn't ready to reveal her secret and part company, all businesslike. She was falling in love with him. More time would confirm her feelings, and she could test out her new and wishful theory that Wyatt was getting over his late wife's death. Silly her. At the very least, she could bide her time and try to find the exact right moment to tell him she was carrying his child.

He lifted his eyes to her. "My mother isn't easy."

"I can handle her."

"She's got a mouth on her."

"So do I."

His gaze dipped to her lips. "Lord, I know."

She smiled.

"She's impetuous, rude sometimes, and likes to get her way."

"Sounds like my kind of girl."

"She'll drive you crazy."

"I won't hold it against you."

"You're determined then? You want to do this?"

Brooke nodded.

"I mean, hell… I'd be lying if I said I didn't want you here longer."

That was encouraging. "Ah, but if I stay, Wyatt, we can't…"

"Yeah, yeah, I get it. I agree. It won't be easy."

No, it wouldn't be easy going to bed at night, knowing that forbidden pleasure and the satisfaction of being in Wyatt's arms were just down the hallway.

Wyatt rose from the bed, shedding the sheet, and stood before her, fully aroused. "You think we can pull this off?"

Her bones melted. She wanted him so badly. She gulped air and nodded. "Yeah, I think we can. It's only for a week, right?"

"Yeah, a week should convince her." He sighed. "Now I'd best get me a cold shower. Seems I'm gonna be taking a lot of those from now on."

Seven

The stage was set. The sun had come out. The land was dry. The roads were clear. All was back to normal.

Well, sort of.

To Genevieve Brandt, Brooke would be Brooke Johnson, the newly hired nanny. The very best Wyatt had ever found. The twins loved her. She had all the right credentials. Wyatt made her a promise to take care of any probing questions his mother might ask when she arrived.

Brooke wasn't a liar by choice. In fact, she hated people who bent the truth to suit their needs. And wasn't she sliding right into that persona now, pretending to be someone she wasn't? In essence, she was also fibbing by omission to Wyatt, too.

By the end of the week, she promised herself, one way or another, Wyatt would know the truth about her pregnancy and all would be settled. A shiver ran through her. She was in deep now and she would have to wade through the days hoping to convince Genevieve that the babies were in good hands. Hoping that Wyatt would...what? Beg her to stay?

Her cell rang and she muttered a choice word as she glanced at the screen. Putting pep in her voice, she answered the call. "Hi, Dylan. How's it going?"

"How's it going? I'm sitting here in my trailer, trying to read lines, wondering why the hell my sister is spending the week with a total stranger. A man with two kids, no less."

"Oh, I explained it all to Emma when I picked up some of my clothes yesterday. He's a good guy really. You know him. He's the consultant to the film. Wyatt Brandt. The storm struck while we were having dinner and I sorta got stuck here."

"It's not raining anymore. Aren't you coming back to Zane's place?"

"Well, as I told Emma, I'm staying here helping him with his twins this week. It's a long story, but trust me, I'm fine."

"Is this a paying job?" Dylan knew damn well it wasn't.

"Hey, I'm a big girl, Dylan. I can take care of myself."

"It's not a job. Oh, right, because you have a job waiting for you back home in California. Are you forgetting that we're leaving for home in less than two weeks? So what's really going on, Brooke?"

"Nothing. God, Dylan. Please, back off. I...kn-know what I'm doing. I'm helping someone out."

Her brother's overprotective groan traveled through the receiver. "All right, I'll back off. I'm only looking out for you, you know."

She sank into the bed Henrietta had made sometime while Brooke was feeding Brianna and Brett their lunch. "I know. I'm... I'm going to be fine." Even to her ears, she sounded uncertain.

"I'm trusting that you are. But I want to hear from you every day, Brooke."

"I'll call. I promise to check in with you and Emma."

Dylan grunted his farewell, and after she hung up, she was torn between loving Dylan to death and wishing he wouldn't treat her like a child. She was twenty-six years old, for heaven's sake. And yes, granted, she'd had a tough year and he didn't want to see her hurt again, but that might happen anyway. Regardless.

The sound of tires crunching gravel on the road put her on alert. She rose and walked to the window. Outside, Wyatt was opening the Jeep door for Genevieve. At first glance, Brooke's eyes widened. Wyatt's mother was beautiful, with sterling platinum hair and a tan complexion complemented by just the right amount of makeup. Wearing a blue silk blouse, a flowing crepe scarf, cream slacks and ankle boots, Genevieve looked every bit the part of New York high society.

Bolstering herself with a pep talk, Brooke headed toward the nursery. Brett and Brianna fidgeted in their cribs, waking from their naps. Just in time.

Brooke made fast work of cuddling them with hugs and kisses, then diapering and changing them into clean clothes. Brianna wore a pink dress with ruffles at the skirt, and Brett wore a new pair of blue jeans, à la Wyatt Brandt, and a little man shirt in red. She was just putting a bow in Brianna's hair when she heard footsteps on the polished wood floors.

"My babies." Genevieve rushed into the room—her pleasant floral scent following her—and picked up Brett immediately. She smothered the boy with kisses, and Brett, love his soul, watched her carefully, as if trying to piece together who this woman was exactly. Genevieve turned to Brooke, looking her up and down. Had she passed the test? "And how's my little Breezy Peezy doing?"

"She's on the verge of being a crank pot. I think she woke up too soon from her nap." Brooke held a fussing Brianna to her chest. "Hello, I'm Brooke," she said to Genevieve.

Genevieve's chin rose. "Wyatt tells me you're good with the children."

From behind his mother, Wyatt shook his head, his lips twitching. Brooke wasn't fazed. She'd dealt with tough cookies from her Parties-to-Go business. "We think alike."

Genevieve laughed. "Do you, now?" She ruffled Brianna's light blond locks and bent to kiss her cheek. Anyone with that much love shining in her eyes couldn't be that bad. "I'm Genevieve. Their grammy."

"Nice to meet you, Grammy Genevieve."

"You can call me Mrs. Brandt."

On the other hand…

"Mom." Wyatt pushed into the room. "Brooke doesn't have to—"

"No, it's okay, Mr. Brandt," Brooke said, giving him a big smile. His eyes bugged out and she almost laughed. They hadn't spoken about what she should call him, but now, it was clear in her mind, she needed to distance herself from him while Grammy was here. "I most certainly will call you Mrs. Brandt. It's not a problem. I was guessing it might be confusing for Brett and Brianna. There's so many names being jostled about, but I'm sure the twins know exactly who you are."

"Of course they do," Genevieve said, just as Brett kicked away from her, reaching for his daddy's arms.

Wyatt grabbed his son and Brett immediately turned his head into his daddy's chest. Genevieve's confident expression slipped a little. "Well, they may need a little reminder," she said. "It's been too long. I miss them."

"I'm sure they miss you, too," Brooke said, swaying her

hips and rocking Brianna side to side. "Bri, would you like your grandmother to hold you now?"

Brianna didn't make up her mind right away, and Mrs. Brandt began smiling and encouraging her. "Come on, Bri Bri. Grammy will rock you."

Genevieve clapped her hands, wiggled her fingers and twirled around in a circle. "And I don't mean on my hip. Wanna dance, Breezy Peezy?"

Brianna giggled, the sweet sound penetrating the tension radiating off Wyatt's body. He needed to lighten up. His mother wasn't all that bad. A bit huffy and pretentious maybe, but she did love her grandchildren.

"Maybe we can all dance," Brooke said, handing Brianna over to her grandmother and giving Wyatt a big nod as she began singing a Taylor Swift song about shaking it off. Wyatt grinned for half a second and began to move. He wasn't light on his feet—that was for sure—but he did have good moves elsewhere. And she loved that he didn't balk at the idea of acting silly with his kids.

The children cackled as they moved throughout the room.

Just then her stomach notched up, a weird kind of hollow, dull ache pulling her out of the dance mentally. Was this what morning sickness was like?

And wasn't that supposed to happen in the morning?

Then she remembered Emma telling her it can hit at any time, day or night. Something would set it off, the smell of food or too much activity or nothing at all. It would just sweep in and make you feel like you could empty your lunch at any second.

Lucky for her, Genevieve put a halt to the fun, claiming fatigue, and Wyatt showed her to her room. It was the second master suite down the hall. Henrietta had told her that after the Brandts retired to the East Coast, Wyatt had a contractor tear down walls in two rooms and construct his very own master suite. The house was certainly large enough for two master bedrooms, and Wyatt had wanted to keep his mother's room intact. Or as Brooke imagined, Genevieve wouldn't have it any other way.

Henrietta walked into the nursery carrying folded baby laundry. Brooke's savior. "Oh, um, Henrietta, can you watch the babies for a few minutes?"

"Of course." Henrietta had gentle eyes and a kind heart. Brooke had only met her yesterday, but she could tell the woman was a nurturer. And loyal to the Brandt household. She didn't know the truth—the less deceit the better—yet she had to be suspicious of how Wyatt had pulled a new nanny out of his cowboy hat over the weekend. But she hadn't said a word about it. Instead she'd readily accepted Brooke, probably greatly relieved to have additional help.

The children were playing with giant interlocking blocks on the floor. Well, munching on them was more like it, giving them a good toothy chew. Henrietta set the laundry aside and squatted on the floor. "Oof."

If Brooke didn't get out of this room immediately, the three of them would witness her double over. "I promise I'll only be a minute," she called, racing out of the room. She sprinted to her bathroom, leaned up against the wall, her hand on her tummy, and took deep solid breaths, praying she could hold it together.

Minutes later and lucky for her, the need to empty her stomach had passed. Only slight tremors rocked her belly now. She splashed water on her face, took a comb to her hair, pulling it back into a ponytail. She felt much better now. She opened her bedroom door.

To Wyatt. He blocked the doorway, his hand fisted, ready to knock. Her jaw dropped and he seemed quite pleased that he'd startled her.

"Wyatt, I'm sorry, I can't talk to you right now. I've got to get back to—"

He shoved at her chest and followed her as she stumbled into her room. He gave the door a quick kick and it quietly clicked behind him. The next thing she knew, she was pinned to the back of the door, Wyatt's hands on her wrists, his beautiful face inches from hers, wearing a wry smile. "I'll show you *Mr. Brandt*," he whispered. And then his mouth was on hers, hungry, possessive and wild.

God, payback was a bitch. She should've known he wouldn't let that go. Her bones liquefied instantly and she kissed him back with a fire that started from deep inside her belly. She was helpless to push him away. "We can't," she pleaded blandly, between kisses. "Your mother—"

"Is locked far away in her room, probably already napping."

Was the locked part wishful thinking? "But the children?"

"Henrietta is doing fine with them."

"But we agreed…"

He nibbled on her throat and then ran his tongue down to her collarbone, taking bites there, too. The secrecy of meeting him like this was a turn-on, but then so was *he*— anywhere, anytime. Just one touch from him turned her brain to jelly. "I'm breaking the agreement. Just for now."

"Wyatt," she sighed, giving in to sensations driving her crazy. They groped at each other like teenagers hiding out behind the stairwell.

If only her teen years had been this exciting.

Finally she put a stop to it. Wyatt, breathing heavy, clunked his forehead to hers. "I don't want my mother bullying you."

"Is that why you came in here?"

"Yes. No."

Something about his confusion tugged at her heart. He wanted her, and that gave her all kinds of happy butterflies, but he wasn't ready and he was clearly battling with his emotions. "I've got your mom pegged already, Wyatt. She's not all that. I can handle her. Now, I've got to get back to the twins."

She made a move, but his hands were still splayed around her waist, and he didn't let go. He gave a yank and their bodies met, thigh to thigh, hip to hip, pulse to pulse. He kissed her once more, a killer kiss that left her trembling. His gaze sharpened on her, a hot blaze of blue lashing her as he opened the bedroom door. "*Mr. Brandt* is leaving now."

Then he walked out of the room.

The land was dry enough to take the children outside. Lord knew, they all had cabin fever. Getting out of the house for some fresh air seemed like a great idea. Until Mrs. Brandt got wind of it and decided to come along.

"Too bad my son couldn't join us today," she said, pushing the double stroller toward the stables. "We could've spent some time together, just the four of us."

Brooke let the comment pass. In Genevieve's eyes, she was just the nanny and didn't rate in a family outing. Wyatt had a meeting this morning and he wouldn't be back from Beckon until later this afternoon.

It was silly how much she missed him. They'd spent the entire weekend together and it had been like a dream. But reality was staring her in the face now. "I'm sure you'll be able to have more time together before you leave. I think Mr. Brandt would like that. I used to love family outings with my folks."

"You're from Ohio, right?"

"Yes, born and raised there."

"Do you have any siblings?"

"Just one brother. Well, technically, we're not related, but we're as close as any brother and sister could be. I was in the foster care system and then was adopted by the...

the Johnson family." Eek. She didn't want to expand on the lies. "But my family is solid and tight. It was my lucky day when Mom and Dad took me in and then adopted me."

"I did some charity work for the foster care program. It appears the system worked for you."

"I was one of the lucky ones. My good friend was in the system and wasn't as lucky as I was, but she's doing well now. She married my brother and life is good."

"Is that why you became a nanny?"

"Oh... I guess. And because I adore children. I babysat my way through high school."

"Madelyn was the same way. She adored children. It breaks my heart that the twins will never know their mother. Wyatt was crushed when she died."

"It had to be rough."

"She was a sweet girl, the perfect match for my son." Sadness seemed to steal Genevieve's breath. "I still can't believe she's gone. A horrible tragedy. Wyatt wouldn't have made it through if it wasn't for his children. Madelyn was the love of his life. He had no choice but to go on."

Such strong words. Oh, to love someone so much that you didn't want to live without them. Yeah, Wyatt would feel that way about Madelyn. Brooke had no delusions about what she was up against. She couldn't fault Wyatt's mother. But she had no idea how hurtful it was hearing her go on about Madelyn. Genevieve couldn't possibly know what Wyatt meant to her.

They walked in silence the rest of the way, the thick-wheeled stroller bumping over rougher terrain, keeping the twins quiet until they reached the stables and a white-fenced corral. Playful horses nudged each other, then raced around the perimeter in an equine game of tag.

"Horsey," Brett called out the second he spotted them.

Brianna followed the direction of his pointed finger and bounced in the seat of the stroller. "Horsey," she squealed, too.

Brooke laughed at how animated they'd become. They lived on a ranch and probably saw the horses every day, but that didn't seem to diminish their enthusiasm.

"Mrs. Brandt, if you'll get Brianna out, I'll get Brett. Henrietta packed carrots. We can show the kidlets how to feed the horses."

Mrs. Brandt chuckled. "The kidlets?"

Brooke shrugged. "I nickname everyone."

"Heavens, don't tell me what name you've picked out for me."

"I promise I won't."

Mrs. Brandt gave her a sideways glance, and then chewed on her lip to keep from smiling. "You have one for me already?"

She was rescued from answering when a tall man in jeans approached. "Is that you, Genevieve?"

Wyatt's mother whipped around and appeared startled. "Oh, uh, hello, James."

James was about the same age as Genevieve, and the hair under his black hat was almost the same silvery-pearl tone. A goatee shaped his chin and jaw and looked marvelous on him. He stared at Wyatt's mother for almost five full seconds, his green eyes sparkling. "Hello."

Brooke made herself busy taking Brett out of the stroller.

"And who is this young lady?" he asked.

"Hi, I'm Brooke. I'm the twins' nanny." With Brett on her hip, she walked over to shake his hand.

He took her in from top to bottom and nodded. "James. I'm the foreman here on Blue Horizon."

"Nice meeting you."

"'Bout time Wyatt saw fit to hire himself a decent nanny."

"Th-thanks. We were just letting the children get some fresh air and hoped they could feed the horses."

"Sure thing," he said, his gaze going back to Genevieve. She did her best to ignore him.

Brianna made noises, stretching her arms up, and James bypassed Genevieve to lift Brianna out of her confinement. "There, there, now, Brianna. Uncle James has you now." He bounced the toddler in his arms and Brianna reached up to pull at the hairs of his goatee, as if she'd done it a dozen times.

Rich, deep baritone laughter poured out of him, the sound amazingly sensual, and Wyatt's mother began fidgeting with the collar of her blouse.

"Don't you have work to do?" she asked, her tone ice-cold.

"Well, now, I've done all that needs doing so far." His chest expanded and he dug his heels in where he stood. "Like always." He bounced Brianna again and she cackled.

Oh, wow. He wasn't a man to be put down by the likes of a strong-willed woman. Watching James with her grand-daughter, Genevieve looked lost for a moment, her light aqua eyes filled with something…longing or regret? It was sad in a way, but it wasn't any of Brooke's business.

"Here, let me have her," Genevieve said to James, putting her arms out.

"Grammy needs a hug," he whispered to Bri and when he made the transfer, his arm brushed Genevieve's— maybe deliberately, Brooke couldn't be sure. Wyatt's mother sucked in a breath and stiffened her body.

"I get plenty of hugs," she barked at him, cradling the baby to her chest.

"Not enough, I'd bet." He stared into Genevieve's eyes and for a moment, Brooke felt as if she needed to give the two of them some privacy so they could hash out whatever they really needed to say to each other.

"Brooke, you said there were some carrots?" Genevieve

needed an escape from James's intense gaze, and the excuse of feeding the horses came to the rescue.

"Oh, yeah. Let me get them." Brooke reached for the bag under the stroller and by the time she had the carrots sorted out and ready, James had said a quick goodbye. She caught Genevieve watching his retreat, her gaze on his backside as he sauntered into the stable.

Wyatt's mother turned around, her face flushed. It was hard not to notice...or comment.

"I'm a good listener, if you want to talk about it," she said quietly.

"There's nothing to talk about." Genevieve's eyes flashed in cold defiance, a reminder for Brooke to mind her own business. There *was* something to talk about, but just not with the family nanny.

Brooke recovered quickly and handed Genevieve a few carrots, then grabbed a few for herself. "Shall we?" They walked over to the corral fence. The horses had a sixth sense when it came to treats, and they'd wandered over, nudging each other to get to the carrots.

"Here you go, Brett. Hold it out," Brooke said.

Genevieve followed suit, giving little Brianna instructions.

"You know your way around a ranch." Brooke was impressed at Genevieve's ease with the animals.

"I know horses," Genevieve said. "And cattle for that matter. My husband saw to it that I knew everything there was to know about his business. God, I loved him, but ranching wasn't in my blood the way it was with him."

It was obvious Genevieve's tastes were far more refined. She wasn't one for living out on a remote ranch, gorgeous as it was, without people, nightlife and high fashion.

"But I miss these babies. And my son." She stroked the bay's mane gently. "Though I think he'd rather not have me here."

It was a confession that surprised Brooke. "I don't think that's true."

Genevieve shook her head and chewed her lip, most likely regretting letting that nugget of information slip. Maybe Wyatt didn't want his mother here right now, but James sure had his eye on her. From all indications, he'd probably like her to stay on at the ranch indefinitely.

Genevieve reached into her pocket and unfolded a hand filled with sugar cubes. "Watch this, Brett and Bri." She put out her hand and moved from one horse to another feeding them the sugar. Afterward, she graced each horse with a loving pat on the head. "Sugar cubes are like cupcakes to horses," she said. "Who here likes cupcakes?"

Brett and Brianna grinned and shouted, "Me! Me!"

"Well, maybe tonight, Grammy will give you some, if you eat a good dinner."

Brooke smiled at the joy on their faces.

So far, so good.

The twins' accidental nanny hadn't blown her cover.

Brooke's tummy heaved and bile rose in her throat. Henrietta had insisted on cooking liver and onions for dinner, and the steamy aroma filled the entire room. Apparently, it was a Brandt family favorite. Lucky for Brooke, the housekeeper also fried up a plate of chicken fingers for the twins. Okay, so she wouldn't starve; she'd eat with the children. But the pungent smell and onion was doing a number on her. Blood drained from her face, and she imagined she'd turned a pale shade of avocado right then.

She wanted so badly to put her hand on her stomach, to somehow make it feel better. But standing near Henrietta and Genevieve, two women who'd carried a child, she feared that gesture would be like drawing a bull's-eye on her belly.

Instead she rubbed at her forehead.

"Something wrong?" Wyatt asked, coming up from behind. She hadn't seen him enter the kitchen.

She gave him a half smile. "Just a little headache."

Struck by the concern in his eyes, she put her head down. "I'll be all right in a minute."

"Why don't you go lie down?" he said.

"Yes, dear," Henrietta said. "I think between the three of us, we can manage the twins. Dinner will keep."

Darn right it would. If she ate a bite right now, she wouldn't be able to hold it down.

"Are you hungry?" Wyatt asked.

"Not really."

"Then go lie down. There's headache medicine in your bathroom."

He glanced at Henrietta and she nodded.

Wyatt, Henrietta and even Genevieve had sympathetic expressions on their faces.

"Okay, but just for a little while. I'll get the twins their baths and put them to sleep later."

"Take the night off. I can do all that." Genevieve seemed eager to spend precious time with the children.

"Thank you, Mrs. Brandt."

Wyatt's lips went tight. He wasn't a fan of his mother's insistence on formality.

"I'll walk you up," Wyatt said.

"No, no. That's not necessary." She gave Wyatt a solid, don't-argue look, and he relented. "Thank you," she said to everyone.

She made her way up the staircase and entered her room none too soon, flopping on the bed facedown, and closed her eyes. Getting away from the ungodly smell of liver and onions was half the battle. She immediately felt less nauseous and was grateful she hadn't made a spectacle of herself in the kitchen. She gave herself up to rest.

A gnawing ache in her stomach woke her and she

snapped her eyes open to darkness. She waited a second for her eyes to adjust to the barest glimmer of moonlight streaming into her bedroom. Slowly, she sat up in the bed and got her bearings. The bedside clock read midnight, and another grumble of her stomach reminded her she'd gone to bed without dinner.

Now she was famished.

She rose and walked into the bathroom. Under dim light she washed her face and changed out of her wrinkled blouse. She ran a brush through her unruly hair, then wove the strands into one long braid, letting it fall down the middle of her back.

Barefoot, she ambled down the hallway and peeked in on the twins. She smiled at their peaceful sweetness and air-kissed both of them. The rest of the house was equally quiet. Carefully, she tiptoed down the stairs and into the kitchen, bracing herself for the awful scent of liver. Thanking all things holy, she was happy to find that the horrid scent was gone. Instead the kitchen smelled sweet, and she remembered Genevieve had promised to bake cupcakes for the twins. The aroma of chocolate was a much better scent, but she wouldn't dare. She opted for a piece of French bread, no butter.

She sat at the kitchen table with the bread and a glass of milk.

"Want some chicken to go along with that?"

She jumped in her seat, startled by Wyatt's voice. "My God, you scared me half to death."

He grinned. "Sorry."

"Why don't you look sorry?"

"Because I heard a noise and was hoping it was you."

"You mean, you'd rather face me than a burglar?"

"I'd rather face you, period."

Oh, wow.

He grabbed a chair, turned it backward and straddled it.

His feet were bare, his jeans riding low. A T-shirt stretched tight over his arms and chest, exposing his solid strength. He didn't look like a filthy rich billionaire, but a father of twins with a bad case of drop-dead gorgeousness.

"Sorry about the meal tonight. Liver's a staple around here. I'll make sure Henrietta doesn't cook it again while you're here."

"Thank you."

"How's your head?"

"My head?"

"You had a headache."

"Oh, I slept it off and then woke up hungry."

"Well, eat up."

She nodded and chewed for a few seconds, aware of Wyatt's gaze resting on her.

"How was your day with my mother?"

"It went well."

"Really?"

"Really." She wouldn't tell him that Genevieve had been curt at times and seemed out of sorts when James showed up. "We took the babies for a walk and I met some of the crew and your foreman, James." She searched Wyatt's face hoping for a clue about his relationship with Genevieve. "He seems comfortable around the babies. Brianna adores him."

"He's a good man, likes kids. He's been with us for twenty years."

"Hmm." She took a swig of milk.

"I bet my mother wasn't thrilled to see him."

She snorted and milk spewed from her nose and mouth. He chuckled. "That bad?"

She nodded her head and grabbed the napkin Wyatt offered. Dabbing at her mouth, she kept her thoughts to herself.

"Ah, that's what I was afraid of. It's no secret James is

smitten with my mom. They dated once, last year when she was here for a visit. James was over-the-moon happy and then Mom called it off. She didn't want to have anything to do with him after that."

"Do you know what happened between them?" She was dying to know. It was a great diversion from her own problems. And maybe she could help.

"I have my suspicions. Mom likes James, a whole lot. And that's the problem. He's a threat to her life in New York. If she got seriously involved with him, it would mean moving back to Texas."

Brooke mulled it over for a few moments. From what she gathered about Genevieve, it made perfect sense. "Maybe that's exactly what she needs, Wyatt. She misses the babies very much, and being near you."

"Ah, but she made her choice when she pulled Dad away from the ranch as soon as he retired. I think she believes it would be a step backward if she gave in to her feelings now."

"So James, I take it, isn't a pushover. He gave her grief over it, right?"

"That would be my guess."

She nodded. Now she understood Genevieve's reaction to James today.

Wyatt took hold of her hand, lacing their fingers together. It was clear the conversation about Wyatt's mom was over. Tingles ran up her arm, and her mind got a little fuzzy.

"Come into my study with me, Brooke," he whispered, leaning close. She suppressed the urge to run her hands through his thick hair. "I want…us."

God. She squeezed her eyes shut. She wanted "us," too. It was wrong. They'd made an agreement. While she was here as his nanny, they had to keep their distance. And yet, as she glanced at their entwined hands, the power of his simple suggestion was a pull she couldn't resist. She wanted to be with him. He excited her and made her long for more. They shared a child, and whether he knew it or not, the bond was there, nestling inside her.

She nodded.

A gleam sparked in his eyes and he smiled, pushing all her female buttons. He stood to pull the chair out for her. Then he grabbed her hand and gave a squeeze as they ambled down the long hallway that led to his study.

With a *click*, they were locked in.

"The babies?" she whispered.

"We'll hear them if they cry out."

And then his mouth was on hers and his kisses washed away all her worries and doubts. Within minutes, they were naked on a wide comfy leather sofa. Atop her, his body was steel to her softness, his chest rock solid as it grazed her tender nipples, his hands threading through the braid that had come loose. In haste and urgency, they explored and pleasured each other in the near-darkness. Wyatt spoke sweet words, loving her body, offering her anything she wanted. He wanted to please her, to make it good for her. The gesture made her fall deeper under his spell.

She loved him.

It was not a big surprise. She'd been falling steadily. He was the kind of man a woman didn't forget. Wyatt made her see and feel the difference between the superficial kind of love she felt for Royce and the love she had for him. He was a real man. A good, kind, solid man, and she had fallen head over heels in love with him.

She rode the wave of his passion, giving him all she had to give, making it good for him, too. When they were joined, his flesh deep inside her, she felt safe. Protected. The connection was real, and not just physically. They shared something wonderful, a compatibility and understanding that carried over to their day-to-day living. She'd never felt more encouraged than now. The urge to speak the truth and get it all out in the open was never stronger. Tonight was the night she would tell him about the baby she carried. His baby.

The joy in her heart led to a wild, furious release. Wyatt joined her, and they shared the amazing climb together, the grind and arch of their bodies in complete sync with each other. "Let go, sweetheart," he rasped, his voice tight and tense.

"Wyatt," she moaned, and the pressure rose to an extreme high.

Both shuddered. Both cried out. Both were bathed in sweat and heat. And then they both came down, Wyatt cupping her head and bestowing kisses on her face.

She'd never been happier.

And afterward, when they were poking around in the dark, retrieving their clothes and attempting to dress, she whispered, "I can't find my panties."

Wyatt chuckled. "It's all part of my plan."

"Wyatt!"

"Hold on a sec," he said, and scrambled for the light switch. Soon the dark study was awash in dim light. And oh, if only her panties weren't missing. If only she could've walked out of that room blindly and gone on with her plan.

But clarity was a bitch. Clarity brought pain. Clarity made her see what she didn't want to admit. Wyatt's study, his most private place and the room where he relaxed and retreated to whenever he needed an escape, painted a very telling picture. There on all four walls, the fireplace mantel, the massive desk and bookcase, were dozens upon dozens of framed photos. Madelyn smiling into the camera. Madelyn riding a horse. Madelyn pregnant with the twins. Madelyn in her bridal gown. The two of them, the four of them, the entire Brandt family. Everywhere.

Yes, she'd seen photos of Madelyn in some rooms in

the house. Henrietta said Wyatt wanted to make sure the babies never forgot their mother. Brooke got that. It was understandable. She'd worry if there were no pictures around of his wife and the mother of his children.

But *this*? The room Wyatt considered his sanctuary wasn't merely a study, but a cluttered cathedral meant for worshipping at the altar of Madelyn. *This* was a wall-to-wall depiction of their life together. Every photo, every scene, every unabashed smile told the story of their love.

His love. For his late wife.

Brooke's mouth gaped open and every good thing inside her fizzled like the bubbles of stale champagne. Her shoulders slumped in defeat.

"Brooke." Wyatt reached for her.

She jerked away. "Don't, Wyatt," she breathed in a hush. "I've been a fool."

"No," he said. "You're not a fool."

She found her panties and finished dressing. "Oh, yes, I am. I get the picture now. Literally. How could I not? I can't do this anymore." She lifted her chin to Wyatt's baffled expression. What did he think? That she'd be overjoyed seeing his devotion to his dead wife? Did he think she wouldn't be affected by his homage to Madelyn Brandt, the true love of his life? "We need to stick to the original plan. While I'm here acting as nanny, we need to keep our distance. And this time, I mean it. Don't come looking for me, Wyatt. Got that?"

He stood facing her, his hands on his hips and his mouth pulled tight, refusing her an answer.

"Do you understand?" she asked.

"Let me explain."

"This," she said, gesturing around the room, "is all the explanation I need."

She spun on her heels and exited the study.

Nausea kicked in big-time. Her stomach gurgled and ached and there was no holding back.

Once she got to her bathroom, she was going to throw up.

Eight

Two days later, the babies sat in their high chairs, making a game of tossing toys off their trays. "Now, now," Genevieve said. "Patience, little ones, we're going as fast as we can fixing your breakfast."

Brooke stirred the oatmeal to cool it down, tossing in some fresh cut-up strawberries.

"There once was a pair of silly twins," Genevieve began in a singsong voice, a deliberate diversion from the great twin toy drop. And sure enough, the children's heads popped up, smiles emerging. "Who liked to *drop, drop, drop* their toys onto the floor." Her voice was lovely, sweet, engaging.

"With a *mop, mop, mop* of curly blond strands," Brooke chimed in singing. "On the *top, top, top,* of their heads."

Genevieve chuckled. Brooke danced the bowls of oatmeal over to the table and took her seat in front of Brett while Genevieve sat down beside Brianna.

"The food goes *plop, plop, plop* into their mouths," Genevieve harmonized.

Brooke giggled and aimed the spoon into Brett's mouth. "And they couldn't *stop, stop, stop* filling their tummies."

Genevieve speared a spoonful into Bri's waiting mouth.

The babies giggled at the rhyming verses, enjoying the silly song and their meal. Once the bowls were emptied and the twins were sipping milk from their sippy cups, Genevieve looked over to Brooke. "You're not half bad, Brooke."

A compliment? "You're pretty good yourself, Mrs. Brandt."

Genevieve chewed on her lower lip, giving Brooke a thoughtful stare. "You know, I think you were right. We don't want to confuse the babies. Call me Genevieve or Grammy."

"You mean in front of the twins?"

"I mean, always." When she smiled, her eyes lit up. In the last few days, Brooke must have passed some sort of test with her.

"Okay, I will. Thanks."

Genevieve seemed pleased with herself. "Good. Now what are we going to do with these two today?"

The morning sun was at Brooke's back, streaming warmth into the kitchen. "I think it's going to be a beautiful day."

"Fall has arrived. It's a shame to let it go to waste. There's a nice playground in Cahill. And if I'm not mistaken, the diner there is pretty good. We can let the babies play at the park and then God willing, they'll nap while we have a peaceful lunch."

"Sounds wonderful to me." It meant spending the day away from the ranch and away from Wyatt. That was a good thing, because she was hurting. Seeing him day in and day out was difficult. Her heart hadn't stopped aching. She was doing everything in her power to keep her distance. He wasn't making it easy, though. He was always around. He loved his twins and wanted to be Daddy to them at every turn. There were times when she wanted to run into his arms and other times when she wanted to run far and fast in the opposite direction.

His eyes always found hers during meals, and although she kept out of his path she couldn't help seeing him when he popped in to play with the twins, or feed them or help put them to sleep at night. Thankfully, Genevieve unknowingly made a nice buffer. Brooke and Wyatt were rarely alone.

Which was a good thing.

But it also broke her heart.

"Will you tell Wyatt our plans, Brooke? I have some phone calls to make before we leave later this morning. Give me a couple of hours."

"Uh, okay. I'll make sure he knows where we're going today."

Genevieve gave the children each a kiss on the cheek. "I'll see you later, my babies."

Once she exited the room, Brooke rose to help Henrietta with the dishes while the twins were still in a happy mood. The great toy drop began anew, but it kept them occupied in their high chairs while Brooke was busy. At least one good thing had come from Brooke being here: Henrietta wasn't exhausted anymore. The older lady actually had pep in her step.

"Did I miss breakfast?" Wyatt walked in, looking sharp in a blue plaid shirt and faded denim jeans. That particular cobalt color brought out the deep hue in his eyes and Brooke had to force herself to keep from staring. Her heart beat hard in her chest.

"I've got eggs and bacon cooking for you, Wyatt," Henrietta said.

"Thanks, Etta." He approached his babies, giving them

a pat on the head and kissing their cheeks. "Morning, my darlins'. Brooke." He turned to her, his gaze unreadable.

"Good morning, Mr. Brandt."

He winced. He hated the formality but she'd kept it up for appearances. And now she was grateful she had that crutch to fall back on. It was just one more way to keep her distance. Often, over the past few days, she'd wanted to simply tell Wyatt the truth and be done with it. The duplicity was killing her, but she'd made him a promise she would stay until Genevieve was satisfied and left the ranch. She wouldn't go back on her word. Besides, they'd have a lot to work out once he learned about the child she carried, and having his mother here would only hamper the process.

In a very real way, Brooke was trapped here by her lies.

Her stomach grumbled. She hadn't eaten yet, either. But bacon and eggs would only make her sick. Morning smells did a number on her very sensitive tummy lately. Luckily, her stomach wasn't on the fritz all day long. If she made it past breakfast eating bland foods, then she was usually good to go the rest of the day.

"Have you eaten?" he asked.

"I, um, no. Not yet. The babies woke early and seemed hungry. No big deal, I'll have some oatmeal later."

"Have it now. I don't like eating alone."

Henrietta glanced at him. Her brows gathered at his less-than-friendly tone. Wyatt was clearly out of sorts.

"Fine." She gave him a fake smile and Henrietta handed her a bowl of oatmeal, then dished up the bacon and eggs for him. She placed biscuits on the table, too. How did any Texas woman retain her figure with biscuits, breads or muffins being served at every meal? Brooke was tempted to grab a biscuit and slather it with butter, but thought better of it. Her tummy could only hold so much food, and oatmeal was the far better choice.

"Would you like cinnamon or sugar with it?" Henrietta asked.

"I'm good with this. Thanks."

After she served them, Henrietta exited the kitchen mumbling something about getting down the fall decorations.

Great, now they were alone. Well, except for the babies. Brooke put her head down, concentrating on eating her oatmeal.

"When I said I didn't like to eat alone, I didn't mean this."

"What?"

"You're giving me the silent treatment."

"It's for the best," she whispered.

"Depends on who you ask."

"Wyatt, don't."

"I'm sorry, okay. It was really a dumb move on my part bringing you into that room."

She bit her lip and looked away. Taking her in there in the heat of passion was one thing, but that his shrine to Madelyn even *existed* was the heartbreaker. Seeing his private sanctuary put everything into perspective. He had every right to hold on to his love for his late wife. But why did he have to make love to Brooke as if it meant something to him? Maybe he shouldn't have made love to her at all. "I don't want to talk about it. Okay?"

He sucked in a breath and then sighed. "Okay. Listen, I want to spend some time with the twins this morning. I'd like to take them for a ride."

"A ride? Where?"

"On the grounds."

"In your car? That seems silly."

A smile emerged, transforming his sulky face. "Not in the car. On horseback."

"You've got to be kidding."

He glanced at his children, who were beginning to wiggle and squirm in their high chairs. "Nope. I rode my first horse when I was one year old. Got the pictures to prove it. If you ask me, they're overdue."

"Okay, suit yourself."

"I'll need help."

"James or your mother could probably help."

"I need your help. Mom's not much for riding and James is too busy today."

"Wyatt, I can't ride a horse."

"You've never ridden before?"

"I have. That's not what I meant. I'm not exactly an expert." She was pregnant. She shouldn't get atop a horse, should she?

"You don't have to be. Do you think I'd risk my kids' safety? I have all the rigging to keep them and you from any danger."

"Well, we can't do it today. Your mom and I are taking the twins into Cahill."

"When?"

"In a couple of hours."

"That gives us more than enough time."

Holding Brett in his arms, Wyatt motioned for Brooke to climb atop the horse. She came forward tentatively, the hat on her head shading her troubled eyes from morning sunshine. He wasn't being fair to her. As sure as the sun rose in the east every day, he knew it. But once a notion took root inside his brain, he had trouble removing it. He'd dug his heels in insisting on Brooke's being a part of the twins' first ride. Now he couldn't imagine doing it without her.

Since their argument, she was on his mind constantly. She'd sidestepped him every moment of every day since, whenever she possibly could. He'd hurt her without intending to, and if he had a lick of sense, he'd let these next few days pass without interjecting himself more into her life. But he couldn't do it. He had a powerful need to spend as much time with her as possible.

It wasn't a conscious move on his part to include her on the ride this morning. Hell no. But after hearing her singing that silly ditty to his toddlers, something snapped inside him. He'd practically ordered her to share the morning meal with him, and then insisted she ride with him and his babies. When she left the ranch for good, he'd miss her like crazy.

If only he had something to offer her. But he wasn't over Madelyn and he couldn't bear hurting Brooke again.

"Step on up to the mounting block," he said to her, holding the reins. "These two mares are the gentlest in the string."

"I know how to mount a horse, Wyatt."

He ignored her and helped her up into the saddle, his hand on her rear end giving a little push. Brooke lanced him with a look that could cut ice.

He bit back a laugh. "This is Maple. She's five years old and sweet as her name."

"Good to know."

Brooke placed her boots into the stirrups and adjusted her position. "I'll hand Brett up to you. And then I'll put the rigging around both of you. You'll be snug and locked in. Just keep one hand on him at all times."

"Okay, got it."

He handed the baby up and immediately, Brett started kicking up a happy fuss. His smile was worth a zillion bucks. "There you go, boy. You like that, don't you?" Once they were secure, he gave Brett a pat on the head. His kids liked the ranch animals. They had no fear, and Wyatt's chest puffed out seeing Brett take to being in the saddle.

"Horsey, go!"

Brooke cracked a smile. If anyone could get that sour

look off her puss, it was Brett. "Not yet, little guy. We'll go as soon as Daddy says so."

Wyatt lifted Brianna out of the stroller and then holding her tight, mounted his mare with ease. He wrapped the protective rigging around both their bodies and clicked his heels, guiding the horse over to Brooke. "Can you tighten this strap?" he asked her.

Brooke leaned way over, took the strap he offered and gave a tug. "That's perfect," he said. "All set?"

She nodded. "Bri's all smiles, too."

"You both look cute in those hats."

Brooke rolled her eyes. Wyatt was too damn happy to take offense. "I'll lead. Try not to fall too far behind."

"We'll keep up, don't you worry."

"Okay," he said. And off they went.

They left the stables and got as far as the house when Genevieve came running out. "Wyatt! Stop! You can't take the twins without documenting this." She had her cell phone in her hands. "It's their first ride."

God, he hadn't thought of that. "Thanks, Mom. You're right. I wasn't thinking."

"Yeah, that happens a lot with you," he heard Brooke mumble.

He gave her a sideways glance. "Maybe because you make me forgot my own name."

Brooke had no response to that, but he liked the way her face flushed pink.

"Maybe you'd like to take my place, Grammy G?" Brooke called out. "You should be in the pictures, not me."

Grammy G? When had Brooke started calling his mother that? When his mom didn't react to the nickname, he was totally baffled.

"No, no, Brooke. I'm a better photographer than I am a rider. You two go on. I'll get some video of this, too. Bri and Brett, look over here at Grammy."

The children were in awe, being atop their favorite animals. There wasn't a peep out of them as they rode by the stables and corrals. Wyatt's ranch hands stopped what they were doing to wave. The twins giggled and gave a wave back. James had a big smile on his face, too, until he noticed Wyatt's mother standing in front of the house with camera in hand. All joy was wiped clean from James's face and just like that, he marched over to the house.

Whatever was going on between James and his mother, Wyatt was keeping his nose out of it.

"Uh-oh, looks like trouble is brewing," Brooke said.

At least she was talking to him. Lately Brooke had barely given him the time of day, except when it came to something regarding the children. How did he turn out to be the bad guy, while his mother and Brooke were such good buddies now? "Mom can be a lot to handle. James has his work cut out for him."

"I think James is just what Genevieve needs. She just doesn't know it yet. Women need lots of encouragement, especially when their mind is set on the wrong thing."

"Do they now?" Wyatt gave her an intense stare.

"Yeah, uh, never mind. I'm the last one to give advice." She looked straight ahead. "How far are we going?"

He let her comments drop, but logged them into his memory. Brooke was good at giving him a female perspective. "Oh, don't know exactly. The kids are enjoying it. I guess we'll head back when they start to fuss."

They ambled down a path heading away from the grazing cattle toward one of Wyatt's favorite spots on his property. The meadow was a mix of bluebonnets and tall grass. It was pretty scenery. "Here's where my granddaddy came up with the name of the ranch. Sitting on the ground looking out, he said the bluebonnets appeared to meet the sky like a blue horizon."

"Wow, I can picture that. It's lovely here."

"Yep. There's a pond up ahead. We can water the horses."

The twins were amazingly quiet, satisfied and thrilled to be riding. One day, they'd own their own horses, learn how to care for and groom their animals. Learn how to respect them. They had time for that, though. He wouldn't rush them. Hell, he still needed a nanny for them. He had two preliminary interviews scheduled on the day his mother was due to leave the ranch. He didn't hold out much hope; replacing Brooke in any capacity would be hard. She was great with his kids and, well, great overall.

And in two days, his mother and Brooke would be long gone.

He wasn't ready to say goodbye to Brooke, but he couldn't ask her to stay. He didn't want to hurt her any more than he already had. The dilemma plagued his mind, but he had to think of the twins. They needed someone steady and constant in their lives. Someone they could rely on. Henrietta and Brooke weren't an option anymore.

"Lookee, Daddy. Duckies," Brianna said, pointing toward the pond.

Brett got wind of it, too. "Duckies! Duckies!"

Brooke laughed. The joy on her face and the way she squeezed little Brett tight, as if she loved the little guy, tugged at Wyatt's heart.

"I see them. They're swimming and taking a bath."

"They look like the duckies in the book I read to you," Brooke said. "*One, Two, Three Ducks*. You remember, right?"

The twins nodded without taking their eyes off the birds, their smiles brighter than sunshine.

Wyatt hadn't known this much joy since before Madelyn's accident. It was as if they were a family, similar to the ducks swimming in his pond, sticking together, having a fun time. A knot twisted in his gut. He knew better. He wouldn't dwell on what couldn't be. But still...

Fifteen minutes later, they were back at the stables and off the saddles. The twins were pooped and ready for a morning nap.

He carried the heftier Brett over his shoulders, while Brooke carried Bri as they headed for the house. Dust kicked up, stopping them midway on the driveway as a slick midnight blue sports car came to a halt right in front of them.

And Johnny Wilde stepped out of his convertible.

Nine

"So that's Brooke?" Johnny said to Wyatt after they'd put the twins down to nap. Brooke was upstairs getting ready for her outing with his mother and the children. "You finally found someone suitable as a nanny, then?"

Wyatt gave Johnny a thoughtful look here in the privacy of his study. He'd learned his lesson the hard way and removed the shrine of photos he'd had of Madelyn in the room. Now only a few of his favorites graced the wall. "Not exactly."

Johnny was his best friend, someone he trusted, a rancher and part owner of the Dallas-based Wilde Corporation he ran with his brothers. They'd grown up together and once upon a time, Johnny had even had an eye for Madelyn. But Wyatt had won her over.

"What does that mean?" With the twist of his wrist, ice shuffled around in the glass of lemonade Johnny held.

"It means, and I know I can trust you…" He eyed him carefully and Johnny nodded. "Brooke is a woman I picked up on the road. We were both going to the same wedding and her car had broken down and...well, it's a long story."

Johnny leaned forward in his chair. "You got my attention at *Brooke is a woman I picked up on the road*. Trust me, Wyatt, for this, I have the time."

Wyatt took a swig of his drink. "I know, it doesn't sound like me, does it?"

Wyatt spent the next ten minutes explaining the situation to his best friend. Johnny listened, keeping his thoughts to himself and nodding.

"So that's it. Brooke is leaving in two days, right after Mom leaves."

"Weird coincidence that she's Dylan McKay's sister."

"Tell me about it. Are you still working on the set?"

"Yeah, part-time. The show wraps in less than a week."

"That means Brooke will be going back to California."

Johnny's dark brows rose and white lines appeared in his otherwise tan forehead. "And you're letting her go?"

Wyatt nodded. "I have to."

"Why?"

"Because I've already hurt her. And I can't... I can't." He began shaking his head. "Listen, you know how hard I took Madelyn's death. I'm still grieving. There's a hole in my heart that will never fill up again. If I got involved with Brooke and it didn't work out, I... I'm just not ready for that."

"Too bad, pal. If it were me, I'd ask her to stay. You said she's great with the kids, and well, if she's that hot in the sack..."

"Watch it," Wyatt warned, his blood ready to boil over. He'd told Johnny that he and Brooke had a good time together. He hadn't elaborated, but it was true, Brooke was hot in bed. Yet hearing it come out of Johnny's mouth rankled him no end. "Don't make me sorry I confided in you."

"Okay, okay. Mellow out, Brandt."

"It's just that, Brooke is…"

"Special? Amazing? Beautiful? Oh, yeah, I noticed."

"You only spoke with her for two minutes."

"Two of the best minutes of my life."

Wyatt gave a half groan, half laugh. "Johnny, you're hopeless."

"I'm just trying to help. If you've got feelings for her, Wyatt, don't run from them. You may never come across another woman you like as much."

"That's just it, I'm not looking for another woman. I need a nanny for my kids. Preferably someone with warts and knobby knees. Someone who doesn't distract me every second of the day."

Johnny laughed. "Man, you are tortured."

"Tell me about it. Come on," Wyatt said. "Mom's probably downstairs by now. She'll want to see you."

"She's the main reason I came by. I couldn't let your mama leave for home without saying hello."

An hour later, Wyatt and Johnny were in the garage helping Brooke load the kids into their car seats. Johnny gave Brett and Brianna high fives and then kissed them on their cheeks. "I'll see you next time I come by, kids. Love you both," Johnny said. "Brooke, it was very nice meeting you."

"Same here, Johnny."

"What do you mean, *next time*? You're staying for dinner tonight," Genevieve said. "I haven't seen enough of you today and the twins would love to see more of their Uncle Johnny. Wyatt, didn't you invite Johnny for dinner?"

"Yeah, Wyatt," Johnny egged him on. "I didn't hear anything about dinner."

"You're welcome to stay for dinner," Wyatt droned.

Johnny glanced at Brooke and gave her a big smile. "I'd like that very much."

Brooke smiled back, and Wyatt's jealousy radar went crazy.

"There, it's settled." The queen of England herself would stand up and take notice at his mother's tone. "We'll see you later tonight."

"Sounds good. And hey, will James be sitting down with us? I promised him a visit, too."

"No, James doesn't usually dine with us," Genevieve was quick to point out.

"But I'll ask him to join us," Wyatt said. He wasn't about to throw James under the bus because of his mother. James deserved better treatment. He'd been loyal to the ranch for decades.

"Well, that's just great." Johnny glanced at Brooke, then Genevieve. "You two ladies have a fun outing. I'll see you all later."

Deliberately, Wyatt didn't look at his mother. If she was pissed, she'd aim her wrath at him, and he had enough to worry about lately.

Dinner at the Brandt house tonight wasn't going to be dull.

That was for darn sure.

"Genevieve, your mouth is going to stay that way if you don't untwist it. At least that's what I was always told," Brooke said.

As Wyatt's mother slumped on the wrought iron and wood park bench, her face wrinkled even more. The usually strong woman appeared diminutive sitting next to Brooke. "Sorry, I'm lousy company today."

The children were playing in the park, shoveling sand into a variety of sifters, pails and animal molds. They were getting filthy and having the best day ever. Horsey rides, ducks at the pond and now the sandbox. Brooke loved seeing the joy in their eyes. They were the sweetest kids.

"Why?"

"It's complicated."

"Life usually is." And wasn't that the truth. She was keeping secrets from Genevieve and Wyatt. And one of those truths was beginning to show in the form of a tiny baby bump.

Genevieve nodded. "I like my life. It's full and rich and when I'm helping others, I feel better about myself. I work for charities and foundations and pour my heart and soul into the work. It's what I love. I've made friends. I have a beautiful home in New York."

"Why do I feel a *but* coming here?"

"It's just one big fat *but*. James."

Brooke laughed.

Then Genevieve laughed, too. "I didn't mean it that way. James is…"

"Nice? Handsome? Persistent?"

"Yes, all of it. He and I, well, we began seeing each other and it was marvelous. I mean, we really had a good, good time. But he wanted more."

"And you're afraid to give it?"

"He used to work for my husband. He works for Wyatt now. I mean…what would people say? How would it look?"

"Like maybe two lonely, intelligent people found each other?"

Genevieve smiled sadly. "I don't think so."

"Why do you care what anyone says?"

She shrugged and tears entered her eyes. "I don't. Not really. But it's taken me all this time to get what I really wanted in life—to live on the East Coast, to be part of society rather than being tucked away on a remote ranch. To have friends, go to the theater and enjoy all the city has to offer."

"There are pros and cons to every issue, Genevieve. What if you gave James a chance and found that you were happier than you could ever imagine? You'd be close to your grandchildren and your son. And I'm sure James could be persuaded to do some of those things you enjoy so much with you."

Genevieve's gaze rested on the children playing so heartily in the sand. Little Bri was standing, wearing an accomplished expression and ready to dump the contents of her tiny bucket into a pile. Brett was busy playing with another child's red toy truck. Behind them, a group of older kids were tossing a football back and forth, their laughter and country music filling the park. "I know. I know. All that might be true," Wyatt's mother said. "Lord knows, I'll never have any more grandchildren. Wyatt is through having babies, and I'm missing out on the ones I do have. I'm just...so afraid."

The comment about having babies stuck like a knife in Brooke's heart. Genevieve had just reaffirmed the reason Brooke was being so cowardly. Wyatt wouldn't want their child, and it crushed her to face that fact. How could she tell him? How could she possibly confess her pregnancy knowing how he felt about having more children? "Fear is something I understand. It can stifle you and cause you to make bad choices and wrong decisions."

But Genevieve's reply was interrupted when a football sailed over her head. Brooke saw the wild pass heading straight for Brianna and leaped into the sand, tackling her to the ground and then *thump*! The football smacked the side of her head. Hard. Pain slashed through her temple and her eyes crossed. She closed them until Brianna's cries reminded her that she had the little one tucked safely beneath her body.

"Brooke! Are you okay?" Genevieve came rushing over and Brooke slowly gave her a nod.

"I think so. I'm a little dazed."

"Goodness, Brooke. You saved Brianna. That ball would've really hurt her. Can you sit up?"

"Yes, I probably can." Although everything seemed to be going in slow motion at the moment, with Genevieve's help, she sat up.

Brianna was dazed, too. Then startled by Brooke's quick reaction, she started wailing. "It's okay, Bri. I'm sorry if I scared you."

Brett had gone pale. Any minute now, he'd start sobbing, too. Genevieve cradled both children, hugging them to her chest.

"Gosh, lady. I'm sorry." It was one of the football players. "Are you okay?"

"No, she's not okay." Genevieve's voice carried across the playground. "She was hit by your football. But it would've been worse if my granddaughter took that hit. Why are you playing so close to the playground? You boys should know better."

"Yes, ma'am. Sorry again."

The boy, joined by his friends, grabbed up his football and slumped away.

"My goodness, Brooke. You dived in to save Brianna. I, uh…" Genevieve choked up, shaking her head. "Thank you," she managed in a whisper.

"I just reacted," she said. "I couldn't let anything happen to Brianna."

Genevieve gave her an intense stare. "Are you sure you're okay? Maybe I should take you to see a doctor."

"No. I'll be fine." She touched the sore spot on her skull. Luckily, her arm had come up to partially divert the knock she took to the head. "I'm a little shaken up. You'll probably have to drive us home though."

"Not a problem. Let me get the kids into the car and we'll get you some ice."

One of the mothers from the playground came running

over. "Gosh, I saw what happened. I have an ice pack. Here you go." She handed it to Genevieve. "That was really brave of you," she said softly to Brooke. "Nice tackle. The momma bear in you came out, didn't it?"

She was about to correct the woman. Brianna wasn't her child, but Genevieve didn't give her the chance. "It sure did. I'm impressed."

"Me, too," the woman said. "Well, I hope you'll be all right."

"Thank you."

The woman gave her a sympathetic smile and walked off.

Brooke figured she must be dizzy in the head, because her first thought after that was that she'd managed to impress Wyatt's mother. What would he say to that?

"How about joining me in a glass of wine, Brooke?" Johnny Wilde offered after he'd poured his own glass on the side bar of the dining room. "It'll help heal that injury you took in the line of duty." He gave her a smooth smile, the wine bottle tipped and ready to pour. Thanks to Genevieve, everyone around the table had heard about the incident at the park.

"No thanks, Johnny. I'd better not."

Standing beside him, Wyatt held a shot glass to his mouth and downed the liquor in one swallow.

Brooke looked away. The babies were down for the night and without them as a shield, she had to deal with Wyatt on her own. They'd had a wonderful morning together, taking that ride with the twins. Now he studied her face and head, looking for signs of her injury, no doubt. There was a perpetual frown on his face aimed at her. It was a bit intimidating.

"You sure?" Johnny asked, ready to put the bottle down. "Being the hero of the day has its perks."

"I'm sure. My head is clear and I'd like to keep it that way. Thanks anyway."

When they returned home this afternoon, Genevieve had insisted that Brooke take a nap, while she took over tending to the children. The rest had done wonders. Her head no longer ached. And the bump on her head was teeny tiny, hardly noticeable. Still she felt uncomfortable with everyone staring at her as if she'd rushed into a burning building or something. Her save hadn't been that dramatic, but Brianna would surely have been hurt if that football had knocked her down.

Genevieve was already sipping wine at the far end of the dining room and speaking with James. It appeared to be a civil conversation from the smile on James's face. If a man could beam, he was surely doing it, and Genevieve's occasional quiet laughter was sweet to the ears.

Wow.

During the first course of dinner, glazed walnut and pear salad, Johnny entertained them with stories of growing up with Wyatt as his best friend. They'd gone to high school together and were teammates in baseball and football.

"*Rivals* is a better word," Wyatt was saying. "You were always trying to best me."

"Trying? I always did," Johnny added.

"In whose world?"

"In my world, Wyatt. Don't you remember who ran for more touchdowns? Who had more home runs?"

"I do recall. That would be me. The numbers don't lie. Maybe your recollections need a little tune-up. Check out the stats."

"I bet you still have them."

"They're here somewhere. Madelyn saved them for me." Wyatt's voice quieted.

Johnny's smirk didn't falter. He loved the banter, and the

mention of Madelyn didn't stop him from teasing Wyatt. "If you'd told that girl the moon was made of blue cheese, she would've believed you."

Wyatt didn't smile. Instead he glanced at Brooke, his soft gaze penetrating her defenses. That's all it took: one apologetic look from Wyatt to crumble the walls she'd tried so hard to maintain. He cared about her, she understood that, but it wasn't enough. Not nearly enough.

Genevieve and James rose from their seats to help Henrietta serve the entrée. When Brooke stood to lend a hand, both Wyatt and Genevieve stopped her immediately. "Don't you dare," Genevieve said.

Wyatt's stony stare said the same.

"I'm fine," Brooke said to everyone, but she lowered down in her seat.

"That's the way we want to keep it, right, Wyatt?" Genevieve gave Wyatt a glance and he nodded.

"I'll help, too."

"No need. Your mom and I have this," James said.

Genevieve gave James a smile and off the two of them went.

"Well, would you look at that," Johnny said. "And here I thought Genevieve had no use for good ole James."

Good ole James was a silver-haired, intelligent man of the earth. He was no country bumpkin, and maybe Genevieve was finally seeing his merits. If something good had come from this little deception she and Wyatt were engaging in, maybe it would be that those two were finding common ground.

"Did you have anything to do with my mother's change of heart?" Wyatt asked.

"Me?" She thought to refute it, but that wouldn't be totally true. And she needed to tell as much truth as she could to atone for all the lies. "Maybe. We had a nice talk today. She's a little confused about some things."

"Mom? Confused? She seems to know exactly what she wants."

Brooke shrugged. "I noticed a change in her after what almost happened to Brianna. She's got some thinking to do."

Wyatt blinked at the suggestion that he didn't know all there was about his mother after all. "I suppose. Maybe you saved more than one person today, Brooke."

"Deserving of a Purple Heart," Johnny said, giving her a winning smile. "Or at the very least a pat on the back and a kiss on the cheek."

Johnny leaned over, put his hand on her shoulder and then brushed a kiss to her cheek. It was short and quick, a chaste kiss, yet he'd stunned her. Heat climbed up her neck and one glance at Wyatt's murderous stare at Johnny had a bubble of laughter erupting from her lips. Only Johnny Wilde could get away with something like that.

"What the hell?" Wyatt rasped.

"What?" Johnny feigned innocence and chuckled.

Brooke couldn't contain her laughter, either. But Wyatt was not amused.

The conversation halted when James walked into the room with a sizzling platter of Blue Horizon prime rib roast. "Here we go," he said, setting the platter down carefully in the center of the table. "Wyatt, I'll do the slicing, if you don't mind. And Gen can serve the roast up. Is that okay with you, Gen?"

Genevieve gave him a smile and nodded. "I'd love to."

It was almost comical watching Wyatt struggle to keep his mouth from dropping open. Admittedly, from what Brooke gathered, James and Genevieve hadn't been this civil with each other in quite a while.

Henrietta walked in with a side dish casserole and then retrieved a basket of home-baked buttermilk biscuits. The room immediately filled with mouthwatering aromas.

It was time to concentrate on the scrumptious meal that looked and smelled delish.

With her stomach on the fritz and her head a little sore, Brooke only hoped she could hold it down.

The knock on her bedroom door came at precisely nine thirty. From her bed, Brooke stared at the door, fearing who was on the other side. She didn't want to speak to Wyatt tonight. She had two more days here, and she was trying to make the best of them. Wyatt seemed to have other plans.

"It's me, Genevieve. Are you awake?"

Surprised, she set her novel down and tossed off her blanket. "Just a sec, Genevieve. I'm coming."

She slid her arms into her robe and tied it before opening the door. "Hello."

Genevieve had a helpless look on her face. "I'm sorry to bother you. Do you have a minute?"

"Of course I do. Come in."

Genevieve entered her room and Brooke led her to the pair of wing chairs that looked out onto Blue Horizon property. The night was dark but for a sliver of moonlight. "Have a seat."

"Thanks." She sat.

So did Brooke. "What's on your mind?"

Genevieve tilted her head to one side. "James. We took a walk after dinner."

"Yes, I saw the two of you leave after dessert. So how was it?"

Genevieve inhaled a deep breath. "Wonderful. So sickeningly wonderful, I can't describe it. I, uh, well, I hope you don't mind me confiding in you. I can't imagine talking about this with Wyatt. But James kissed me goodnight and it was beyond amazing. It was bells and whistles going off."

"That's wonderful, isn't it?"

"I hope so. We talked at length and decided to take it slow. But I am going to continue seeing him. Do you think that's the right move?"

"I do, Genevieve. I think taking it slow is a good thing. You can spend more time here in Texas, and maybe he'll come to visit you in New York."

"That's what we're going to try to do. Maybe split our time and see how it goes. It'll give me more time with the twins, too." She nibbled on her lip. "Brooke, is it crazy to do this at my age?"

Brooke smiled. "Not at all. My goodness, Genevieve, if you see what I see when James looks at you, I'd say it'd be crazy not to. If you have feelings for each other, why not explore them?"

Wyatt's mother began nodding, taking in her suggestion. "I don't think I would've come to this conclusion without you."

"Me?"

"You're easy to talk to. I know I can be bitchy at times, but I respected how you managed me."

"You're not bitchy, exactly. And I wasn't managing you."

"Saying how calling me Mrs. Brandt might confuse my grandchildren? That was just the right comeback for me. And well, after your quick reaction with Brianna today, it was like a boulder being dropped on my head."

Brooke rubbed her sore skull. "Make that a football and I'd understand."

"Oh, dear, and I haven't even asked you about your head."

"It's fine. I'm fine. Go on," she said.

"Okay, I won't keep you much longer, I promise. But I wanted to thank you for listening and for your advice today. I have been sort of lost, coming here and seeing James again."

"Well, if I helped you in any way, I'm glad."

"You did. I realized today how badly I want more time with my grandchildren. It all seems to fit now. James and me, more visits to the ranch, less city, more country. I think I can do it."

"I'm happy for you, Genevieve."

"I'm sad I have to leave day after tomorrow. I haven't spent any time getting to know you. It's all been about me. Next time I come out I plan to spend time getting better acquainted with you."

"Uh, well, that would be nice." She felt like a heel, letting Genevieve Brandt believe she'd be here when she returned. Not only wasn't she really the twins' nanny, she was carrying Wyatt's baby and couldn't confide in Genevieve. The woman would probably end up hating her once she found out about all the lies Brooke had told.

What a deep hole she'd dug for herself.

Another soft knock came at her door and she froze. Her heart beat like crazy in her chest. Before her new visitor—more than likely Wyatt—could say something, Brooke called out. "Just a minute!"

Genevieve appeared genuinely surprised. "Who could that be?"

"Probably your son. I promised to give Mr. Brandt my... my schedule for next week. I have to take a few days off and he'd wanted to check with Henrietta to make sure she could cover."

"Goodness, I wish I could help out. I'd love to, but I've had this commitment in Dallas on the books for months."

Brooke swept over to the door. "It's going to work out, don't worry," she said, opening the door to Wyatt's somber face. "*Mr. Brandt*, I'm sorry I forgot to give you my schedule."

Wyatt stared at her as if she'd grown bull horns, and then noticed his mother walking toward him. He scratched his chin, buying time, and finally catching on. "No problem, I just wanted to remind you. And see how you're feeling. Hello, Mom."

"Wyatt. It's late for Brooke. Don't keep her up too long. Gosh, you are so much like your dad. He couldn't go to bed until he dotted his *i*'s and crossed his *t*'s."

"Yeah, the hazards of being a Brandt, I guess."

"Good night Brooke, get some rest." Genevieve patted her shoulder gently and then eyed her son for a moment. "Remember, you can discuss business in the morning."

Wyatt nodded and waited until his mother walked down the hallway and closed the door to her room. Then he sighed. "What was that all about?"

"Mostly about James, but I can't discuss it."

Wyatt didn't press the point. "May I come in?"

"If you have to."

He frowned and stepped inside her room.

Ten

Brooke tightened the ties on her robe and hugged herself around the middle. Wyatt was giving her his signature devilish blue-eyed look that threatened to devour her in one huge gulp. She didn't need any more private time with him. She'd told him to stay away, but he didn't listen very well. "Why are you here?" she asked on a sigh.

He frowned at her bluntness. "I'd like to see your bruise, Brooke."

"Why? The last time I checked, you didn't have 'MD' behind your name."

"Are you saying you need a doctor?"

"No, it's just a bump. It hurt like hell before, but the pain's gone now."

"Well, then. Show me. I couldn't see a damn thing at dinner."

"What's the point of having long hair if I can't cover up my wounds?" She was being deliberately obtuse with him tonight. Because…because, darn him, he was standing in her bedroom like her miracle cowboy again, with doggone sympathy and admiration in his eyes. The two didn't at all mesh, but on him, it looked appealing.

He stood with feet planted wide, hands on his hips, his jaw made of granite. "How bad is it?"

"Oh, for heaven's sake, Wyatt." She stepped closer to him and under a halo of lamplight angled her head slightly, pushing her hair to the side. "See, it's not that bad."

He winced and his breath rushed out. "There's definitely a bump there. Dammit. I wish to God you hadn't gotten hurt."

She believed him, because Wyatt was a decent man. That was the good news and the bad news.

"I told you at dinner, I'm fine now."

"What you did for Brianna…" He shook his head as if he couldn't find the words.

"I'm happy she wasn't hurt," Brooke said softly. "There's no need for you to be here worrying about this."

"Thank you for protecting her."

"You're welcome."

"You're making it impossibly hard for me to find a real nanny, you know."

"You're just saying that because your mother likes me."
I even impressed her today.

"You're likeable, but Mom never takes a shine to people this quickly."

"She's not that bad, Wyatt. I feel terrible lying to her about all this."

"Just for another full day. Then she'll be on her way."

Brooke backed up a step and stared into his eyes. "And so will I."

Wyatt cleared his throat and nodded. "I know. Brooke, listen," he said, his voice deep and raspy. He came toward her, all iron-jawed handsome, and she closed her eyes.

"Don't, Wyatt."

"There are things I need to say to you. Things that need explaining."

"Look, you're off the hook, okay?" She smiled, softening her words. "I don't need to hear all about your heartache and your undying love for your wife. I don't need you to say nice things to me. I'll be leaving soon and…and…"

I'm having your baby.

God, it was on the tip of her tongue. But she held back. In less than forty-eight hours, she'd be gone from Blue Horizon. She needed more time before she told him. She needed to gain some perspective. She needed to discuss her situation with Emma and Dylan. Why hadn't she done that yet? Why had she jumped in with both feet without seeing how deep the bottom was? Without knowing how far she would fall?

Her decision made, she walked to the door and opened it. "Wyatt, I'm tired. I really should get to sleep."

"All right," he said, striding to the door. "Good night, Brooke," he said quietly, and then landed the softest kiss on her cheek. "Sleep well."

She gazed into his eyes. "You, too."

He shot her a dubious look, as if the last thing he would do was get a good night's sleep. He left her at the door and sauntered away. She fixed her focus on his retreating form, all cowboyed up, tight-jeaned and hunky.

Then she closed the door and put her hand to her tummy as tears spilled down her cheeks.

Brooke sat cross-legged in the great room among wooden alphabet blocks, dolls and two little people cars, playing with Brianna and Brett. The twins were a lot of work, but they were also adorable and sweet and Brooke's heart broke thinking she'd be leaving them tomorrow. Not only had she fallen for Wyatt, but she'd fallen for his kids, too.

"Here you go, Breezy Peezy." She handed Brianna a red block.

Brianna flung it across the room.

"No, we don't do that."

Brett giggled and it only egged Brianna on. She picked up another block and tossed it as hard as she could. It nearly hit Wyatt's gazillion-inch flat-screen TV. "Bri. No!"

She grabbed Brianna's hand and the little girl's face turned cherry red and she broke down in sobs. "Oh, it's okay, Bri. It's okay. Come here." Brooke cradled her in her arms, absorbing her genuine, honest-to-goodness tears. They soaked her blouse.

She'd been having so much fun playing with them, she didn't realize their nap time had come and gone, and the twins were both on the verge of hysteria.

Wyatt walked into the room, took one look at Brooke with Brianna and then scooped up Brett. "Nap time."

"Yeah, it's overdue. My fault."

His eyes warmed on his daughter and he ruffled her hair. "They're just having too much fun with you. It's hard not to." He kissed the top of Bri's head and she immediately stopped crying. "You're gonna be okay, sweetie." Then he planted a kiss on Brett's head. "Up we go."

They climbed the stairs and entered their nursery, his compliment humming through Brooke's system. "My mom thinks it's time for the babies to have their own rooms."

Brianna had nearly conked out in her arms during the climb up the stairs. Brooke lowered her down gently and the little one curled her body up, nestled down and fell fast asleep. "Well, I've told you before, I don't think there's any rush. You can do it in a year or so when they develop different tastes."

"You mean like blue for boys and pink for girls?"

She chuckled quietly. "Only if it's their choice. Boys

do tend to prefer trucks and tractors over princesses and castles. At least that's how it worked in my family."

He nodded. "So you think I've got some time? They've had so many changes in their young lives, I don't want to make things harder on them."

"Yes, I think there's time."

"Book?" Brett's tiny voice rang in her ears.

"I'm here," she whispered. It was so cute how the babies called to her.

He put out his chubby arms and Wyatt made the transfer. Brett liked the way she rocked him to sleep. She bounced him up and down, to and fro, and slowly his inquisitive blue eyes closed. She laid him down.

"You're good for my kids," Wyatt said, almost as if he was thinking aloud.

Brooke bit down on her lip to keep from crying herself. She'd been weepy lately, and only part of it was due to her pregnancy. She left the nursery and Wyatt followed her into the hall.

"I'm taking Mom out for dinner on her last night here. James is going and I'd love for you to join us," he said.

"Oh, Wyatt...no, I don't think so. I'll stay home and watch the twins so you can have a peaceful meal."

"The babies are coming. It's nothing fancy, but it was my mom and dad's favorite barbecue place."

"Suddenly, I have a craving for barbecue again," Genevieve said, walking up to them. "And I insist you join us, Brooke. It'll be fun."

"Oh, uh?" What could she say; it was two against one. "Okay, sure."

"I'll drive with James and you and Wyatt can bring the twins."

Three hours later, the four of them were seated in a booth at the Brickhouse, James sitting next to Genevieve and Wyatt next to Brooke. She was as close to him as she wanted to get tonight, breathing in his incredibly rich scent of musk and lime. At times, they brushed shoulders. At times, they brushed thighs. It was hard not to react. Hard to pretend there wasn't more between them. Being here with his family, it dawned on her she really didn't fit in. She wasn't part of the love they shared. Even James belonged here more than she did. He'd known the Brandt family for decades.

A pitcher of beer sat on the table, and all three of them had offered at one time or another to pour her a glass. She shook off their attempts, claiming to prefer lemonade to quench her thirst.

But when the ribs were served, with coleslaw, mashed potatoes and corn soufflé, oddly, her stomach didn't rebel. She dug in as heartily as the others. "Mmm, this is good."

"I knew you'd like it," Genevieve said.

"How long have you been coming here?" Brooke asked.

"Since the place opened," Genevieve said.

"I think it's going on forty years, right, Mom?"

Genevieve smiled. "I worked here as a hostess."

"You did?" James seemed to eat up anything he learned about Genevieve. "I didn't know that."

"It was only for a few months. But I got to eat all the free food I wanted. It was my first job."

They shared a sweet glance.

"My first job was mowing lawns in Ohio. Hostessing sounds like more fun," Brooke said.

The babies were indulging in mashed potatoes and cut-up chicken tenders.

Everyone seemed content.

Until Brooke looked across the restaurant and nearly spit out her lemonade. There, seated in a booth in the far corner of the place, sat Dylan and his very pregnant wife, Emma. Dylan's disguise, a cowboy hat and thick glasses, might fool some, but Brooke would know her brother any-where. She froze in her seat. She couldn't panic. Think-ing fast, she glanced at Wyatt. "Uh, would you excuse me for a second? I need to use the restroom." She shrugged. "Too much lemonade, I'm afraid." TMI, too, but it couldn't be helped.

"Sure thing." Wyatt scooted out of the booth and she slid out after him.

"Thanks."

She strolled down the aisle and hoped like hell no one at the Brandt table was watching her. Luckily, she heard the twins begin to whine and grumble, which usually drew all attention their way.

Thankful the restaurant was crowded, with not a single table empty, she made a quick turn to the left, passed two booths and then scooted in next to her brother. He jumped, his eyes going wide seeing her suddenly sitting beside him. "Brooke? What are you doing here?"

"Same thing as you. Having dinner and hoping not to be recognized." She slid a quick glance at her bestie. "Hi, Emma. How're you feeling?"

"Hungry. Seems I'm always feeling that way lately. It's good to see you, Brooke. We miss you."

"Miss you, too."

"What's all the mystery?" Dylan asked, noting how strange she was acting.

"Shh," she said to both, slinking down in the seat. "Please don't ask why right now, but I don't want the peo-ple I'm with to know I'm your sister. But it's not what you think. Just trust me, okay? I promise I will explain every-thing tomorrow when I come back to Zane's place."

"You sure you're okay?" Dylan asked, giving her a good once-over with his eyes.

"Yes, I swear everything's fine."

"And I would know that, if you called me every day like you promised."

Emma came to her defense. "Dylan, she's called me several times since she's been gone. We know she's doing well. You have to trust her."

Dylan shot his wife a baffled look and then sighed. "Fine, then. I'll see you tomorrow."

"Thanks. Oh, and nice disguise, Dylan."

She slid out of the booth quickly, before he had time for a snarky comeback, and leisurely strolled back to the table.

Disaster averted.

As she sat in the kitchen enjoying the morning sunshine, Wyatt came in, surprising Brooke and disturbing her peace. He sauntered inside with that lazy *I'm Texan* way he had of getting her attention. Wyatt's presence always seemed to surround her, even when he was ten feet away. "Mornin'," he drawled.

"Good morning."

He homed in on her sipping hot cocoa and nibbling on a slice of toast. She'd hoped to have a few moments of solitude before the household woke, but instead she found herself gazing into the clearest blue eyes she'd ever seen. So blue it hurt her heart.

"I'm gonna be driving my mother into Dallas today."

"I know." She'd dreaded this conversation.

He slid into the seat facing her and leaned in real close. "I don't know how to thank you for all you've done." He reached across the table and took her hand.

"There's no need." She glanced at the door. Genevieve or Henrietta could walk in any minute.

"There is a need. You've been amazing in so many ways, Brooke. And you've meant something to me."

Would he care to name that something? No, she didn't think so. It wouldn't be what she wanted to hear anyway. She reached for a napkin with the hand he'd held and dabbed at her mouth. It was a way to break the connection without being totally obvious.

"We're all going to miss you."

"I'll… I feel the same," she said, setting both of her hands in her lap. No sense tempting fate. She couldn't bear to have him take her hand again. It was hard enough gazing into his eyes and knowing things would never be the same between them. "I feel bad leaving the twins with Henrietta. She does so much already."

"It won't be for long. I've got two interviews today that look promising. Whoever I hire could never replace you, but we'll make it work."

"I'm glad, Wyatt. Really. And you know, if your mother moved back to Texas, it wouldn't be the worst thing in the world," she said quietly.

"Yeah, I know. That's a long way off still, but I'm going to build her a cottage on the property. It's something she and Dad had always talked about. They drew up the plans and everything. So, if she wants to come back, she'll…" He cleared his throat. "She'll have some privacy."

Brooke smiled. "That could be the best of both worlds."

"If only everything was that easy." He kept staring at her, his voice husky. She would embed that voice in her memory bank.

She didn't feel much like finishing her toast. And this conversation was just about over. They'd said all there was to say to each other. "Well, I've got some packing to do myself," she said, standing. Wyatt immediately stood, too. "I'll say goodbye now. I'll be gone before you get back."

He stood silently and studied her. There was no *stay and give us more time together* or *I don't want you to leave.*

No, Wyatt only sighed, nodded his head and stared at her lips so long she thought they'd catch on fire. And then he leaned in and kissed her. As far as kisses went, this one was subpar. It was a cautious, someone-might-burst-into-the-room kind of kiss that spoke to Wyatt's unending sense of propriety and decency. It was one of the traits she loved most about him. He always did the right thing, no matter what.

Her eyes stung. Tears threatened. She had to make a clean break and get out of here before she confessed all of her sins and told him she loved him. "Goodbye, Wyatt."

And then she marched out of the room, her head held high, her face perfectly masked in a performance worthy of an Academy Award.

Later that afternoon, with a hole in her heart and missing the twins and their father like crazy, Brooke entered Zane's magnificent custom-built home with two pink bakery boxes in hand. She had a lot of explaining to do, and sugar always seemed to help.

"Hello? Anyone home?" she called out. She might as well get this over with, but on the drive from the bakery in Beckon, she suddenly felt lighter, the weight lifted, knowing she was about to unburden herself of the truth.

"We're out here," Dylan called from the backyard.

She found Dylan and Emma stretched out comfortably on chaise longues on Zane's veranda overlooking the countryside. They sipped from tall glasses of iced tea. "Hello, my family," she said.

"Ah, the prodigal sister has returned bearing gifts, I see," Dylan said.

Emma rolled her eyes. "Hi, Brooke. What did you bring us?"

"A peace offering," she squeaked.

"And why do you need a peace offering?" Dylan asked as he sat up on his chair, all jest aside.

"Because I have a confession to make and it's a big one."

Dylan and Emma exchanged glances.

"I've got red velvet cupcakes for you, Em, your favorite. And for Dylan, I brought an assortment of bakery cookies."

It was a throwback to when they were kids. Dylan had an eye for only the best, even then. He longed for the better decorated, fancier cookies he'd see displayed at the local bakery on his way to school every morning. But Mom couldn't afford the luxury, so she brought home the grocery store brand every week. When Dylan finally made it big, he began sending home fresh-baked cookies on a regular basis to their folks.

"Raspberry shortbread?" he asked.

"And chocolate-dipped macaroons. Take a peek," she said, holding open the box.

Not only did he peek, he grabbed two and gave one to Emma. "These are the best," he told her.

Emma chuckled. "You're like a little boy getting his favorite cookie."

"You're my favorite cookie," he said to her with a wink. "Brooke, take a seat, have a cookie and tell us your big confession."

She lifted a shortbread cookie out of the box and sat down. "Hmm. I've been *craving* these." She bit down and the soft cookie crumbled in her mouth.

"Craving?" Emma asked, scooting up in her lounge chair. "As in the way I have cravings?"

There was another exchange of looks between her and Dylan.

Brooke nodded. "Let me start from the beginning. You see, I met my miracle cowboy on the road to Heather's wedding..."

When Brooke was through telling her story, shedding her guilt about hiding the truth from them and begging for their understanding about the baby, Emma wrapped her up in her outstretched arms. Brooke snuggled into her embrace and breathed a sigh of relief. "Brooke, of course we understand. And to think, our babies will be very close in age. They'll be cousins."

The acceptance in Emma's voice did wonders. "Yeah, that part is exciting."

But Dylan sat pensive, staring at her, absorbing all the facts. "This guy's got to be told he's the father of your child, honey. If he's as decent as you say, he'd want to know."

"You're right, Dylan, he should know, but I'm… I'm in love with him. And he's still grieving over his late wife. The love of his life," she said quietly. "I've heard him say half a dozen times his two children were quite enough. He doesn't want any more. I don't think I could take seeing disappointment or fear enter his eyes when he learns the truth. I wanted to tell him the entire time I was staying there, but…it just wasn't the right time."

"You were too busy playing nanny to his kids and deceiving his mother," Dylan replied.

"Dylan, please." Emma rose to her defense. "We both know some things are out of our control. Brooke did what she thought was right at the time."

Her brother ran a hand down his face. "God, I'm sorry, sis. I just wish you would've come to us first."

"You're right. I should have confided in you guys. I know I've handled this whole situation all wrong. I was hoping…"

"Hoping what?" Dylan asked.

"That Wyatt would fall in love with her," Emma answered.

Brooke gave her friend a nod. No more needed to be said. Heartsick, she choked up. Wyatt had said goodbye to her. He hadn't stopped her from leaving. He didn't love her.

Her bestie had her all figured out. It was most likely because a similar thing had happened between her and Dylan. For a time, Dylan thought the baby Emma carried was his, and when he found out the truth he'd been taken by surprise and deeply hurt. But he came to love both Emma and the baby with all his heart. They were one tidy little family unit now and happy as clams.

Dylan came over and pulled Brooke into his arms. She rested her head on his broad shoulder and felt his love surround her. He really was the best brother ever. "We'll work it out, hon. Don't worry." He stroked her hair and kissed her forehead.

"Thanks. I feel better now that you know the truth. But I'm unsure what to do next."

"Give yourself a day or two," Emma said. "You need to be away from the situation for a while. I'm sure you'll figure out what to do."

"I'm gonna tell him, Em. Maybe just not to his face."

"Just don't text him," Dylan said, trying for levity.

"Maybe I'll send him an email."

Dylan tugged on her hair. "You're a goof sometimes. You know that?"

"Yeah, I know that."

Emma took her hand, and Dylan held her around the waist. The three of them were solid. "We're here for you, Brooke," Emma said.

"If you need something, just let us know," Dylan added. "You're feeling well?"

"Yes, just a bit of morning sickness, but it's not terrible."

"Good," Emma said. "It should pass soon."

"My shoot's almost over. Just a few pickup scenes and we're done and headed home. Don't rush into anything," her brother said. "Take Em's advice and think things through."

"I will. I promise. I already feel ten times better now that you guys know. Thanks. Your support means so much to me. Now I think I need a nap. Confessing is exhausting."

"Have at it, sis. We'll be here when you wake up."

"I think I'll take a nap, too," Emma said. "Our baby might grow up to be a soccer player with all the kicking he was doing last night. I didn't get much sleep."

"It's dangerous, you know," Brooke said, starting to feel her old snarky self again.

"What is?" Emma asked.

"Leaving Dylan alone with that entire box of bakery cookies. He might get pudgy around the middle and then the ladies won't buy tickets to see his movies."

"Funny," he said, reaching for the box, but Brooke was too quick for him. She snatched it up, tossed him a sole macaroon and then strolled away with the box under her arm as she headed for her bedroom.

"You're the one who'll be getting pudgy around the middle," Dylan called to her.

She grinned and thanked heaven for normalcy again.

Well, as normal as her life could possibly be from now on.

Without seeing her miracle cowboy every single day.

Wyatt sat atop Josey Wales, his favorite gelding in the string as the sun descended on the horizon. Riding had always been his balm, a way to cool off from a bad day, a way to let off steam. He'd pushed his horse hard this evening, racing against the sunset, going farther and farther out on Brandt land. Now that they'd turned around, Josey was taking his sweet time heading back to the house.

It was a lonely time of night. The babies were already asleep, thanks to the new nanny he'd hired just today, Loretta Martinez. She didn't have warts or knobby knees. Her résumé had been the best of the women he'd interviewed. Loretta was in her midforties, divorced, a little chubby, and her own children were all grown up. At first, the twins called out for "Book" each time Loretta went to pick them up. It broke his heart all over again that Brett and Bri would have to make another adjustment in their lives. They missed Brooke.

So did he.

He pushed his Stetson back from his forehead and sighed. The ride, the night air and cooler temperatures weren't working. He felt lonesome and isolated, cut off from the world. Abandoned by Brooke McKay. Though that made no sense, since the deal he'd made with Brooke was that she'd stay the week until his mother left for Dallas. She'd honored her part of the deal. He was the one having trouble with all of it.

You big dummy, you didn't ask Brooke to stay. Of course you feel abandoned. It's your own damn fault.

By the time he reached Blue Horizon stables, misery had set in. He dismounted and led the horse inside for grooming. When his cell phone rang, he had a mind not to answer, especially when he saw the caller's name pop up. But it could be important. His mother didn't usually call at night, preferring to FaceTime with the twins while they were awake.

"Hi, Mom," he said.

"Wyatt, what's wrong? I can hear it in your voice. Are the babies okay? Bri didn't catch cold. She was sneezing quite a bit when I left the ranch last week."

"Everyone is fine. I'm just in from a ride and the babies and I are all healthy."

"Okay, good. That's a relief. Actually, I'm looking for Brooke. She isn't answering her cell. Is she there by any chance?"

"Uh, no. She's not. Why do you ask?"

"She promised to give me her recipe for almond crusted halibut. She said it was foolproof and you know how appealing that sounds to me. My cooking skills are lacking lately. I'd like to perfect the recipe for the next time I come out. I'll make it for everyone."

CHARLENE SANDS   177

"You mean, you'll make it for James, don't you?"

"Well, if he likes fish, he's welcome to come."

Wyatt chuckled. His mom was so transparent. "Maybe you can email her, Mom."

"Oh, right. I guess I could do that. Speaking of Brooke, I've been thinking about her, honey. Does she have someone?"

Wyatt cleared his throat. He hadn't broken the news that Brooke had been replaced yet. "Someone?"

"A boyfriend or anything? She never talked about her private life."

"Maybe because she wants to keep it private."

"She's great with the twins, Wyatt. But I couldn't help noticing for such a thin girl, she had a bump in her belly and well, she never touched a drop of alcohol even when she was off the clock. One morning I saw her take a look at the ham and eggs cooking on the griddle and turn pea green. I thought she was going to lose her lunch, right then and there."

"What exactly are you getting at, Mom?"

"Nothing. I'm being silly."

"Mom," he said more firmly.

"She's the best you're going to find as a nanny, Wyatt. I don't want you to lose her because she's pregnant."

"You think Brooke's pregnant?"

"I, um, it's just a hunch, son."

Wyatt ran a hand down his face. His whole body shook at the possibilities. He'd noticed a little thickening of Brooke's stomach lately, but hadn't thought anything of it. To him, she had the perfect body. But if he recalled correctly, Brooke didn't have any trouble drinking alcohol at Blake and Heather's wedding. Yet a month later, while she was there, she'd never accepted a drink from him. Little things were beginning to add up in his head now. All those little remarks he'd made about the twins being enough for him and Brooke giving him strange, almost pained looks after his comments. "Mom, I've got to go. I'll talk to you soon."

He ended the call quickly and slumped against the stable wall. Could it be true? Was Brooke carrying his child? Suddenly, and out of the blue, he came to the conclusion that he didn't need to know. It wouldn't matter anyway.

He pushed Johnny's speed-dial number. His friend answered on the first ring. "Johnny? Tell me what's going on with the production. Are they through filming yet?"

"Hello to you, too, pal."

"Listen, this is serious. I need to know if Brooke is still in Texas."

"Wow. You are serious. Yeah, she should be. As a matter of fact, I'm getting ready to go to the wrap party tonight. The whole cast is supposed to be there. I'm assuming she'll be there, too."

"Where is it?"

"They've rented out the Applewood. Are you crashing it?"

"Damn right I am."

"This I gotta see. Listen, I'll swing by and pick you up in half an hour. Deal?"

"Deal."

Wyatt showered and dressed fast, then began pacing the floor and glancing at his watch every fifteen seconds. When he heard the roar of an engine in front of his house, he was out the door instantly. "Hey, thanks for this," he said to Johnny. "But is it okay if we take my car?"

"Sure, why?" Then his friend caught a glimpse of what was happening over Wyatt's shoulder. "You're bringing the artillery?"

"Have to. I need all the help I can get."

Johnny smiled. "When you say it's serious, you mean it."

* * *

Wyatt walked into the Applewood Bar and Grill, an iconic honky-tonk that rivaled the famous Gilley's. The place was swarming with the cast and crew of Dylan McKay's Western movie. Wyatt spotted a few people he'd worked with on the day he'd filled in for Johnny.

Country music blared, a classic Zane Williams hit about loves lost and found. Wyatt moved through clusters of people chatting, scanned over the bar area and peeked into a small stadium arena where wannabe cowboys pressed their luck on a mechanical bull. There was no sign of Brooke.

He turned around and collided smack into someone's chest. The guy was built like granite and didn't offer an apology for blocking his way. When his gaze drifted to the man's face, he understood the reason. "McKay."

"What are you doing here, Brandt?"

They were nose to nose. "I didn't come for the food or the company. I'm looking for Brooke."

Dylan's chest puffed up with brotherly concern. "You weren't invited."

They could butt heads all day, but Wyatt was beyond that. If he had to make nice to Brooke's brother, he'd swallow his pride. "I know. I apologize. But this is important. I've got to speak with Brooke. Is she here?"

Dylan looked him up and down, his expression grim. "You plan on hurting her?"

"God no. I'm here to…"

"What?"

"To make things right."

"That means different things to different people," McKay said, still eyeballing him.

"You have my word, I'm not going to hurt her. That's all I can say for now."

They stared at each other for beats of a minute and then Dylan nodded. "Okay. I dragged her here, but she wasn't in the party mood. She's in one of the private offices. Follow me."

"No, it's okay. Just point me in her direction. I'll find her."

Dylan moved through the crowd and down a hallway. Wyatt followed quietly behind. When Dylan stopped and gestured to a room with a paneled door at the far end of the hallway, Wyatt made a move to pass him. And Dylan got in Wyatt's face again. "Remember what I said."

He tipped his hat. "Got it."

As soon as Dylan walked away, Wyatt whipped out his cell phone and called Johnny. Then he strode over to the door and knocked, his heart beating in his chest like crazy.

Brooke's eyes were just closing when a knock on the door broke her peace. She jumped and the phone on her lap fell to the floor. So much for the novel she was reading. Another knock boomed and this time, Brooke shook out the cobwebs in her head. "Hang on a second," she called.

Music filtered in, the lyrics muffled through the closed door, yet the sweet melody of the ballad came through softly. The din of conversation told her the party was in full swing. Too bad. She'd been ready to leave hours ago, which was weird, since parties were her business. Literally. Maybe Dylan and Emma had had enough country twang and porterhouse steaks for one night.

She rose and went to the door. "Ready to leave yet?" she asked just as she turned the knob and opened the door.

"Now that depends on you."

Her breath whooshed out as she took in the length and breadth of the man she loved. "Wyatt, w-what are you doing here?"

"Funny, your brother asked me the same thing. I guess I'm crashing the party."

She blinked. She couldn't believe Wyatt was standing on the threshold, one hip braced against the doorjamb.

He took his Stetson off, held it to his chest in true cowboy form and gave her a killer smile. "May I come in?"

"Oh, uh…yes. I guess so."

He walked in and turned to her, his smile wider and his face…well, how could a man get even more gorgeous in just a week's time? She was filling up on the sight of him, allowing her heartsick soul to take him all in.

"You look beautiful, Brooke."

"Thank you."

"Why don't we sit down?"

"Why?" She eyed him cautiously. Why was he here? Why were his sky blue eyes glowing like that? A girl could get her hopes up if she wasn't too bright.

"Because I've got things to say to you. And you're gonna listen. Now sit down."

She frowned.

"Please."

She sat on the cream sofa and he sat down next to her, as in, so close their thighs touched. She swallowed hard, planted her feet and waited.

Wyatt sighed as he set his hat on the sofa and then reached for her hand. It fit so nicely in his, and she trembled from his touch. "The truth is, when I married Madelyn, it was for life. I mean, I loved her so much, I could hardly breathe sometimes. She was everything to me. And we had this perfect little family. I was happier than I thought a man had a right to be. But you already know all that. What you don't know is that when you came into my life, I thought it was a brief interlude. I was instantly attracted to you and fooled myself into believing that it was lust. A simple case of lack of sex and female contact."

She gasped. "Are you insulting me, Wyatt?"

"Not at all, sweetheart. I'm trying to explain. And maybe I'm not doing the best job of it. You'll have to forgive me for that. But the honest truth is, I wasn't afraid to be myself around you, because I never thought I could have feelings for another woman. I never thought I would ever find love again. Certainly not so soon after Madelyn's death. She's been gone less than a year and my mind-set was that I'd be alone for a long, long time. Deeply caring for anyone before that time wasn't an option. But then you became the twins' nanny. Granted, it wasn't real, but it was. Wasn't it? I mean, you care for my kids, don't you?"

"Now I'm the one not able to breathe, Wyatt. Yes, I love those kids. They're amazing and sweet and..."

"They've been asking for Book."

A tear slipped down her cheek. "Really?"

He nodded.

"Are you trying to win me back as your nanny, Wyatt?"

"No. Don't cry, sweetheart. I'm trying to tell you I love you. I mean it. I've fallen crazy in love with you. And it took you leaving and a phone call from my mother to make me realize it."

Her heart bubbled up. "You love me?"

"I love you."

She caught her next tear with her finger and wiped it away. "I love you, too."

He squeezed her hand and then leaned in to give her the best kiss in the entire world. A sweet, simple brush of the lips that sewed her heart up good and tight.

"I want you to marry me, Brooke. I want you to come live with me at Blue Horizon. I want you to be my wife and help me raise my twins. But before you answer me, I want you know that my mother thinks you're carrying a child. She may be all wrong but after hearing what she had to say, I realized that yes, I'd want a child I'd conceived with you, but I'd want you to marry me, regardless. I missed you so much, I could hardly stand it."

He got down on one knee. "So I'm going to ask you again. Whether you are or aren't carrying my child, will you marry me? Oh, and wait one darn second."

He pulled out his cell phone and texted someone.

Really? In the middle of his proposal?

Johnny Wilde entered the room, holding two sleepy-eyed babies in his arms. He set them down and once they spotted her, they waddled right into her arms. "Book, Book."

"Oh!" The babies were here! Her eyes watered again. She scooped them up and kissed each one on the cheek. "I've missed you two."

"Mission accomplished," Johnny said, giving a salute and backing out of the room.

Brooke chuckled between her tears.

"They want you for their mommy, Brooke," Wyatt said. "And I just plain want you."

Brooke couldn't believe her ears. She was hopelessly and fully in love with Wyatt Brandt. And yes, she'd have to make some changes in her life, give up her business or run it long distance, but right now, all that mattered, all she wanted, was Wyatt Brandt and his two adorable children.

"You can answer me anytime now," Wyatt said, still on bended knee.

"Yes, I'll marry you," she said, snuggling the twins. "And yes, I'm carrying your child. I was going to tell you before I left Texas. I truly was. I just didn't know how to tell you to your face. I was afraid you wouldn't want me or the baby."

"It's okay, Brooke. I get it. I didn't make things easy on you. I was stuck in my grief and almost lost you because of it."

"I was wrong not to tell you sooner. I'm sorry, Wyatt. I just couldn't find a way."

"You would've told me, Brooke. I have faith in that. I only wish you would've trusted me more. But I get it. We were both raw and cautious from past hurts."

He took her hand and kissed her fingertips. "You have to know, I'm glad about the baby. *Our* baby. It'll be a fresh start for both of us." Wyatt grinned wide, and Brooke's fears were put to rest with that one gesture, that one affirmation of his true love for her.

"I'm so happy."

"So am I." Then he turned to the twins. "Did you hear that, kids? You're going to have a brother or sister one day soon. There's gonna be more little Brandts running around the house."

"It's going to be a madhouse," Brooke said, grinning and picturing it in her mind.

"I can't wait," Wyatt said.

"Really?"

"Really. I'm good with all of it, sweetheart."

Of course he was.

He wouldn't be her miracle cowboy otherwise.

And Wyatt Brandt was that, and so very much more.

* * * * *

MILLS & BOON®
Hardback – May 2016

ROMANCE

Morelli's Mistress	Anne Mather
A Tycoon to Be Reckoned With	Julia James
Billionaire Without a Past	Carol Marinelli
The Shock Cassano Baby	Andie Brock
The Most Scandalous Ravensdale	Melanie Milburne
The Sheikh's Last Mistress	Rachael Thomas
Claiming the Royal Innocent	Jennifer Hayward
Kept at the Argentine's Command	Lucy Ellis
The Billionaire Who Saw Her Beauty	Rebecca Winters
In the Boss's Castle	Jessica Gilmore
One Week with the French Tycoon	Christy McKellen
Rafael's Contract Bride	Nina Milne
Tempted by Hollywood's Top Doc	Louisa George
Perfect Rivals...	Amy Ruttan
English Rose in the Outback	Lucy Clark
A Family for Chloe	Lucy Clark
The Doctor's Baby Secret	Scarlet Wilson
Married for the Boss's Baby	Susan Carlisle
Twins for the Texan	Charlene Sands
Secret Baby Scandal	Joanne Rock

MILLS & BOON®
Large Print – May 2016

ROMANCE

The Queen's New Year Secret	Maisey Yates
Wearing the De Angelis Ring	Cathy Williams
The Cost of the Forbidden	Carol Marinelli
Mistress of His Revenge	Chantelle Shaw
Theseus Discoyers His Heir	Michelle Smart
The Marriage He Must Keep	Dani Collins
Awakening the Ravensdale Heiress	Melanie Milburne
His Princess of Convenience	Rebecca Winters
Holiday with the Millionaire	Scarlet Wilson
The Husband She'd Never Met	Barbara Hannay
Unlocking Her Boss's Heart	Christy McKellen

HISTORICAL

In Debt to the Earl	Elizabeth Rolls
Rake Most Likely to Seduce	Bronwyn Scott
The Captain and His Innocent	Lucy Ashford
Scoundrel of Dunborough	Margaret Moore
One Night with the Viking	Harper St. George

MEDICAL

A Touch of Christmas Magic	Scarlet Wilson
Her Christmas Baby Bump	Robin Gianna
Winter Wedding in Vegas	Janice Lynn
One Night Before Christmas	Susan Carlisle
A December to Remember	Sue MacKay
A Father This Christmas?	Louisa Heaton

MILLS & BOON®
Hardback – June 2016

ROMANCE

Bought for the Greek's Revenge	Lynne Graham
An Heir to Make a Marriage	Abby Green
The Greek's Nine-Month Redemption	Maisey Yates
Expecting a Royal Scandal	Caitlin Crews
Return of the Untamed Billionaire	Carol Marinelli
Signed Over to Santino	Maya Blake
Wedded, Bedded, Betrayed	Michelle Smart
The Surprise Conti Child	Tara Pammi
The Greek's Nine-Month Surprise	Jennifer Faye
A Baby to Save Their Marriage	Scarlet Wilson
Stranded with Her Rescuer	Nikki Logan
Expecting the Fellani Heir	Lucy Gordon
The Prince and the Midwife	Robin Gianna
His Pregnant Sleeping Beauty	Lynne Marshall
One Night, Twin Consequences	Annie O'Neil
Twin Surprise for the Single Doc	Susanne Hampton
The Doctor's Forbidden Fling	Karin Baine
The Army Doc's Secret Wife	Charlotte Hawkes
A Pregnancy Scandal	Kat Cantrell
A Bride for the Boss	Maureen Child

MILLS & BOON®
Large Print – June 2016

ROMANCE

Leonetti's Housekeeper Bride	Lynne Graham
The Surprise De Angelis Baby	Cathy Williams
Castelli's Virgin Widow	Caitlin Crews
The Consequence He Must Claim	Dani Collins
Helios Crowns His Mistress	Michelle Smart
Illicit Night with the Greek	Susanna Carr
The Sheikh's Pregnant Prisoner	Tara Pammi
Saved by the CEO	Barbara Wallace
Pregnant with a Royal Baby!	Susan Meier
A Deal to Mend Their Marriage	Michelle Douglas
Swept into the Rich Man's World	Katrina Cudmore

HISTORICAL

Marriage Made in Rebellion	Sophia James
A Too Convenient Marriage	Georgie Lee
Redemption of the Rake	Elizabeth Beacon
Saving Marina	Lauri Robinson
The Notorious Countess	Liz Tyner

MEDICAL

Playboy Doc's Mistletoe Kiss	Tina Beckett
Her Doctor's Christmas Proposal	Louisa George
From Christmas to Forever?	Marion Lennox
A Mummy to Make Christmas	Susanne Hampton
Miracle Under the Mistletoe	Jennifer Taylor
His Christmas Bride-to-Be	Abigail Gordon

MILLS & BOON®

Why shop at millsandboon.co.uk?

Each year, thousands of romance readers find their perfect read at millsandboon.co.uk. That's because we're passionate about bringing you the very best romantic fiction. Here are some of the advantages of shopping at www.millsandboon.co.uk:

* **Get new books first**—you'll be able to buy your favourite books one month before they hit the shops

* **Get exclusive discounts**—you'll also be able to buy our specially created monthly collections, with up to 50% off the RRP

* **Find your favourite authors**—latest news, interviews and new releases for all your favourite authors and series on our website, plus ideas for what to try next

* **Join in**—once you've bought your favourite books, don't forget to register with us to rate, review and join in the discussions

Visit **www.millsandboon.co.uk**
for all this and more today!